P9-APF-611

He felt something for her.

A responsibility to protect her. It went deeper than just being responsible for someone he was thrown together with because of fate.

Jack felt something for *her*.

Undoubtedly the feelings he'd experienced had all been brought on by the car accident, and he didn't like the wave of panic that had assaulted him when he'd first heard Gloria screaming. And he definitely didn't like the odd sensation that had waltzed through him, filling every cavity, when she'd clung to him after he'd extracted her out of the vehicle.

Things had stirred inside of him. Things with cobwebs and dust on them.

Feelings.

The last things he wanted awakened within him were feelings. And the sooner this woman was out of his hair, the better.

Dear Reader,

Spring might be just around the corner, but it's not too late to curl up by the fire with this month's lineup of six heartwarming stories. Start off with *Three Down the Aisle*, the first book in bestselling author Sherryl Woods's new miniseries, THE ROSE COTTAGE SISTERS. When a woman returns to her childhood haven, the last thing she expects is to fall in love! And make sure to come back in April for the next book in this delightful new series.

Will a sexy single dad find *All He Ever Wanted* in a search-and-rescue worker who saves his son? Find out in Allison Leigh's latest book in our MONTANA MAVERICKS: GOLD RUSH GROOMS miniseries. The Fortunes of Texas are back, and you can read the first three stories in the brand-new miniseries THE FORTUNES OF TEXAS: REUNION, only in Silhouette Special Edition. The continuity launches with *Her Good Fortune* by Marie Ferrarella. Can a straitlaced CEO make it work with a feisty country girl who's taken the big city by storm? Next, don't miss the latest book in Susan Mallery's DESERT ROGUES ongoing miniseries, *The Sheik & the Bride Who Said No*. When two former lovers reunite, passion flares again. But can they forgive each other for past mistakes? Be sure to read the next book in Judy Duarte's miniseries, BAYSIDE BACHELORS. A fireman discovers his ex-lover's child is *Their Secret Son*, but can they be a family once again? And pick up Crystal Green's *The Millionaire's Secret Baby*. When a ranch chef lands her childhood crush—and tycoon—can she keep her identity hidden, or will he discover her secrets?

Enjoy, and be sure to come back next month for six compelling new novels, from Silhouette Special Edition.

All the best,

Gail Chasan
Senior Editor

Please address questions and book requests to:
Silhouette Reader Service
U.S.: 3010 Walden Ave., P.O. Box 1325, Buffalo, NY 14269
Canadian: P.O. Box 609, Fort Erie, Ont. L2A 5X3

Her Good Fortune

MARIE FERRARELLA

SPECIAL EDITION

Published by Silhouette Books

America's Publisher of Contemporary Romance

If you purchased this book without a cover you should be aware
that this book is stolen property. It was reported as "unsold and
destroyed" to the publisher, and neither the author nor the
publisher has received any payment for this "stripped book."

Special thanks and acknowledgment are given to
Marie Ferrarella for her contribution to
THE FORTUNES OF TEXAS: REUNION series.

To Patience Smith, my Guardian Angel,
with sincerest thanks

 SILHOUETTE BOOKS

ISBN 0-373-24665-X

HER GOOD FORTUNE

Copyright © 2005 by Harlequin Books S.A.

All rights reserved. Except for use in any review, the reproduction
or utilization of this work in whole or in part in any form by any
electronic, mechanical or other means, now known or hereafter
invented, including xerography, photocopying and recording, or in
any information storage or retrieval system, is forbidden without
the written permission of the editorial office, Silhouette Books,
233 Broadway, New York, NY 10279 U.S.A.

All characters in this book have no existence outside the imagination of
the author and have no relation whatsoever to anyone bearing the same
name or names. They are not even distantly inspired by any individual
known or unknown to the author, and all incidents are pure invention.

This edition published by arrangement with Harlequin Books S.A.

® and TM are trademarks of Harlequin Books S.A., used under license.
Trademarks indicated with ® are registered in the United States Patent
and Trademark Office, the Canadian Trade Marks Office and in other
countries.

Visit Silhouette Books at www.eHarlequin.com

Printed in U.S.A.

Books by Marie Ferrarella in Miniseries

MARIE FERRARELLA

This RITA® Award-winning author has written over one hundred and thirty books for Silhouette, some under the name Marie Nicole. Her romances are beloved by fans worldwide.

Pssst, have you heard?
They're baaack!

Silhouette Special Edition presents three *brand-new* stories about the famous—and infamous!— Fortunes of Texas. Juicy scandals, heart-stopping suspense, love, loss… What else would you expect from the fabulous Fortunes?

Beginning in February 2005, read all about straitlaced CEO Jack Fortune and feisty Gloria Mendoza in RITA® Award-winning author Marie Ferrarella's *Her Good Fortune,* Special Edition #1665.…

Then, in March, Gloria's tell-it-like-it-is older sister, Christina Mendoza, finds herself falling hard for boss Derek Rockwell's charming ways, in Crystal Green's *A Tycoon in Texas,* Special Edition #1670.…

Finally, watch as youngest sister Sierra tries desperately to ignore her budding feelings for her best friend—and emotional opposite— Alex Calloway, in Stella Bagwell's April installment *In a Texas Minute,* Special Edition #1677.…

The Fortunes of Texas: Reunion
The price of privilege. The power of family.

Prologue

"All right, what's wrong?"

Maria Mendoza looked up from the items she was straightening on the counter. On it was displayed a multitude of skeins, her latest shipment of angora yarn. The veritable rainbow of colors appeared as cheerful as she was sad. Maria had hoped that keeping busy in the shop would dispel the darkness that insisted on dwelling inside of her. After all, this was her shop and it had become successful beyond her wildest expectations.

But none of that did anything to lift her mother's mood.

"What makes you think something's wrong?" With effort, she put on the best face she could for the dark-haired woman who had entered the shop.

Rosita Perez, her cousin and dearest friend in the whole world, frowned. "You and I have known one another for more years than I will willingly admit to anyone except for Reuben," she said, referring to her husband. "I know when there's something wrong with you. You look as if you've lost your best friend." Rosita, older by four years but shorter by several inches, picked up a skein, as if debating whether she needed or wanted more wool, then replaced it. "And as far as I know I'm still breathing."

Maria shook her head. "No, not my best friend, my daughters." Then, because Sierra still lived within Red Rock's city limits, she clarified, "Christina and Gloria," although there was no need. Rosita was as aware of the girls' location as she was.

Rosita placed a comforting hand on her shoulder. "Maria, this isn't exactly anything new. The girls have been gone five years—"

"Exactly." Maria sighed, struggling against the overwhelming sadness. "Five *years*. With no end in sight. This is not why I became a mother, Rosita, to hope for an occasional word from my daughters." She splayed her hand over her chest. "There's a hole in my heart."

"You've still got Sierra and Jorge close by," Rosita pointed out. She tactfully omitted mentioning Roberto, who'd moved to Denver, the same city that Gloria had chosen to disappear to.

"And a hole in my heart," Maria repeated. Even if

she'd had a dozen children, she'd still feel the lack of the two who had left. Roberto returned frequently, Gloria and Christina did not.

Rosita shrugged, spreading her hands wide. "So, plug it."

Maria blew out a breath. Her cousin made the situation sound so simple. "How?"

Rosita wandered from display to display within Stocking Stitch, which was what Maria had chosen to call her store. "Get the girls to come home."

Maria's impatience continued to grow. She stepped in front of her cousin before Rosita could move to yet another display. "Again, how?"

Rosita shook her head. "I have never known you to be slow with ideas, 'Ria. You could throw a party."

Of course, how could she not have thought of that? Jose would cook, as he always insisted on doing, and she could be the hostess. Nothing made her happier than to have everyone home, under one roof. Maria smiled. "A big party."

"A big family party," Rosita agreed.

The smile faded from Maria's lips. She was deluding herself. "But the girls will pass when I ask them to fly out. This thing between them…" She had never gotten all the details, but it wasn't a stretch for her to guess at what was going on. Christina, her oldest, and Gloria, her wild one, had had a falling out. Most likely over a man. "There're bad feelings."

Rosita remained unfazed. The two had spent many

hours talking about their children. "So? Come up with something to block out these bad feelings."

A smile took hold of Maria's lips, melting away the years. By everyone's standards, she was still a very handsome woman. "I could tell them that their father's had a heart attack. They'll come rushing back for that."

"They'll come rushing to the hospital," Rosita pointed out. "That's where they'll expect to see him if he's had a heart attack."

Maria nodded. Rosita had a point. "Chest pains, then," Maria amended. "We'll hold a family reunion and I'll tell the girls that if they miss this one, I don't know if their father will be here for the next one." She looked at her cousin, a sunny smile on her lips. "What do you think?" she asked as she picked up a pad and pen from the counter.

"I think that I'm happy we're friends and not competitors."

But Maria didn't hear her. She was busy making notes to herself for the party she and her husband were about to throw.

Chapter One

Like an outsider staring through a one-way mirror, Gloria Mendoza Johansen looked slowly around at the people milling about and talking in her parents' spacious living room. Everyone seemed to be enjoying themselves.

Just like the old days, she thought.

There were people in every room of the house, confined inside rather than spilling out onto the patio and the grounds beyond because of the cold weather. February in Red Rock, Texas, left its mark. At times raw, it could leech into your very bones.

But inside the house, everything was warm, cozy. The way she had once thought the world was. But she'd learned differently.

As she floated from place to place, observing, hesitating to join in, she twirled the stem of her glass. A wineglass to hide the fact that she was drinking seltzer instead of something alcoholic.

Because she was one.

A recovering alcoholic, to be exact. Except that alcoholics never really recovered, she thought wryly. They were doomed to an eternal dance, always careful to avoid the very thing that they would always, on some level, crave. A drink. But she had been sober two years now and she was determined to remain that way.

Nodding and smiling, she didn't pause to talk to people who looked inclined to engage her in conversation. She was still picking her time, taking it all in. It felt strange coming home. In part, it was as if she'd stepped into a time warp and five years had just melted away, never having passed.

But they had passed.

They'd left their mark on her in so many ways. Too many for her to think about now. Besides, there really was no point.

Go forward, don't look back.

It was something she told herself almost daily, a mantra she all but silently chanted within the boundaries of her mind. And now, finally, she was beginning to adhere to it.

"They're your family. They won't bite, Gloria. Mingle."

Her mother. She'd caught the scent of her mother's

perfume a beat before the older woman had said anything.

Gloria glanced over her shoulder at the diminutive woman. At sixty-two, Maria Mendoza still had the same figure that had first caught Jose Mendoza's eye, no mean feat after five children. She was wearing her shoulder-length black hair up tonight. The silver streaks added to the impression of royalty, which was in keeping with the way she and the others had viewed her when they'd been children. It was her mother who had summoned her like the queen mother to return home.

Gloria smiled to herself now. Her mother had no idea that she'd been toying with that very notion herself, not for any so-called family reunion or to come rushing back to an ailing father who in her opinion looked remarkably healthy for a man supposedly battling chest pains, but to relocate. Permanently. To set up her business and her life where it had all once began.

Home.

She'd fled Red Rock five years ago when she'd felt her life spinning out of control, when the effects of alcohol and drugs had all but undone her. She'd thought that if she got away from everything, from her mother's strong hand and everything that had contributed to her feeling of instability, the temptation to drink herself into oblivion and to drug her senses would disappear.

As if.

Because everywhere she went, she always had to take herself with her. It had taken a great deal of soul-searching and one near-fatal catastrophe—her nearly falling off a balcony while intoxicated—for her to finally face the fact that the problem was not external but internal. If she wanted her life to change, then *she* and not her surroundings needed to change.

So she'd shed the poor excuse for a husband she'd acquired in her initial vain attempt to turn her life around and then scrubbed away every bad habit she'd accumulated since she was a teenager. To that end, she'd checked herself into rehab, probably the hardest thing she'd ever done, and prepared to begin from scratch. And to learn to like herself again.

She knew the process was going to be slow. And it had been. Like molasses rolling downhill in January. But every tiny headway she made was also fulfilling. And as she grew stronger, more stable, more certain, she realized that she wanted to return to a place where people—most people, at any rate—liked her.

She'd wanted to return home.

And home was her parents. It was also her sisters, but that hurdle she hadn't managed to take yet. When she'd left, she'd left her relationships with them, especially her older sister, Christina, in shambles.

She still had to do something about that.

One step at a time, Gloria cautioned herself.

She'd gotten everywhere else so far and she'd get there, too. Just maybe not tonight. She'd already seen her sisters, both of them, but from a distance. And that was what she intended on keeping tonight: her distance.

The same height as her mother, except that she was wearing heels that made her almost two inches taller, Gloria inclined her head toward the older woman. "Papa looks terrific for a man who's had a heart attack," she commented, not bothering to keep the smile from her lips.

"Chest pains," Maria corrected, as if the reason she'd given both her older girls had not been a creative fabrication. "I said he'd had chest pains."

Gloria could feel her brown eyes fill with humor as she looked at her mother—and saw right through her. "More like indigestion maybe?"

Maria shrugged her shoulders, dismissing the topic. It was obvious that her mother was not about to insist on the lie. It had done its work. It had brought her home. "He wanted you here as much as I did." Maria fixed her with a look that spoke to her heart. "As I do."

There was no point in keeping her decision to herself any longer. Gloria slipped her arm around her mother's shoulders. "Then I have something to tell you."

But her mother cut her off, as if she was afraid she would hear something that would spoil the moment and the party for her. "Whatever it is, I am sure it is fascinating, but you can tell me all about it after you get my shawl."

Gloria looked at her uncertainly. If anything, the press of bodies made the air warm, not cool. "Your shawl?"

"Yes, I left it in the den." Already turning in that direction, she placed her hands on her daughter's back and gave her a little initial push to start her on her way. "Get it for me, please."

Gloria paused, then shrugged in compliance. Going to get her mother's shawl gave her an excuse to withdraw for a moment. Just because she'd made up her mind to uproot her life for the second time in five years and come back home didn't mean that the idea didn't make her just the slightest bit uneasy. She supposed it was because she kept thinking about that old line she remembered from her high school English class. Some author, Wolfe? Maybe Hardy? Whoever it was had said you couldn't go home again.

She prayed it was just a handy title for a book and not a prophecy.

The immediate reason she'd left Red Rock was that she'd blacked out after a drinking binge only to wake up to find herself beside a man she'd had no recollection of meeting. But in part she'd fled to San Antonio because relations had also deteriorated between her and her sisters. They'd been so close once, but that had been as children and children had a tendency to overlook things adults couldn't.

Such as cutting words and deceptions that should never have taken place. She and Christina had worked for the same financial firm, Macrizon, naive in their enthusiasm. And were easy prey for a woman named Rebecca Waters who took perverse pleasure in pitting one of them against the other.

Maria, looking impatient, ran her hands along her arms. "Please, Glory, I'm getting cold."

She looked at her mother suspiciously. Was she getting sick? But Maria's face appeared as rosy as ever. Again, Gloria shrugged. "Fine, Mama. One shawl, coming up."

She made her way to the den, wondering if her father knew how oddly his wife was behaving tonight.

The second she walked into the den, she knew she had been set up.

Maria Mendoza, you're still a crafty little woman, she thought.

Her younger sister, Sierra, was standing inside the bookcase-lined room, looking around as if she was searching for something. She'd watched as Christina, her older sister, had preceded her into the room by less than a minute.

Gloria shook her head. She should have seen this coming a mile away.

Despite her unease, she couldn't help commenting, "All we need now is a little Belgium detective with a waxed mustache and a cup of hot chocolate saying, 'I know that you are wondering why I asked you all to be here tonight.'"

At the sound of Gloria's voice, Christina whirled around to look at her, her mouth open in surprise. Sierra's head jerked up. She looked as if she could be knocked over with a feather plucked from a duck's back.

Awkwardness warred with that old, fond feeling

she'd once had when she was in the company of her sisters. "Mom sent me," Gloria finally explained.

Lights dawned on her sisters' faces. "Papa sent me," Christina told them.

"Rosita," was Sierra's contribution for the reason behind the exodus that had brought the three of them to this room.

Suddenly, Gloria felt herself being pushed into the room. Catching her balance, she whirled around, only to have the door shut in her face. Her sisters were immediately on either side of her as she tried the doorknob. It wouldn't give.

Big surprise.

"It's locked." Maria's voice came through the door. "And it's going to stay that way until the three of you resolve your differences and come out of there acting like sisters instead of angry strangers."

"You're really going to be needing that shawl, Mama." There was nothing Gloria hated more than being manipulated. She knew her sisters felt the same way about being played. "Considering that hell's going to be freezing over when that happens."

She tried the door again, but it still didn't give. Her mother was obviously in for the duration. Angry, Gloria turned to look at the two other women. Now what? She jerked her head in the direction of the door. "She sounds serious."

Christina snorted, her arms akimbo. "Mama can get pretty stubborn when she wants something."

And that, Gloria thought, was a prime example of the pot calling the kettle black. Gloria eyed her older sister. "You're not exactly a shrinking violet yourself in that department."

It was impossible to read Christina's expression. "And you are?"

Sierra placed herself between the two older women she still loved dearly. Peacemaking came naturally to her, it always had. Becoming a social worker had only intensified that tendency.

Shorter than both her sisters, Sierra nonetheless refused to give ground as she looked from one to the other. "Tina, Glory, let's not pick up where you two left off five years ago."

Edgy, nervous, Gloria felt like the odd girl out. When she'd left, it had been Christina and Sierra against her.

She raised her chin now, defensive, wary. Wondering if the other two were willing to begin again the way she was or wanted to draw the lines in the sand again. "And why not?"

Sierra looked exasperated. She also looked older, Gloria thought. More in control. "Because it's obvious that Mama and Papa want us to pick up where we left off ten, fifteen years ago, not five."

Gloria searched Sierra's face. Her younger sister wasn't just paying lip service to something. It was obvious she was speaking what was in her heart, as well.

A smile slowly emerged on her lips. She continued to test the waters. "We were pretty close then, weren't we? Be nice to just step on a magic carpet and go back in time."

Sierra had a better solution. "Or just forget what went down."

Gloria looked at Christina. The acrimony, because that was what it had become, had been mainly between her and her older sister. It had spilled out onto Sierra only when she'd thought that Sierra had joined forces with Christina against her.

Maybe things wouldn't have seemed so intense, so distorted and so overly dramatic if she hadn't been trapped inside a bottle at the time, Gloria thought. A lot of the fault, if she were being honest, had lain with her.

She offered Sierra a rueful smile, covertly watching Christina's expression. "That's a whole lot of forgetting."

Christina took a deep breath, her natural composure slipping into place. Of the three of them, she was the most unflappable, at least outwardly. The one who seemed to be able to take everything in stride. Not too many people guessed at the chaos going on inside. Or at the pain.

She seemed to reach a conclusion. "I can if you can," Christina finally said, looking at her.

Which put the ball squarely in her court, Gloria thought.

She didn't want to be thought of as the lesser sister, the one who clung to old arguments and hurt feelings. The one who refused to allow bygones to be bygones.

More than anything, she wanted to bury the recent

past and return to the years when they had viewed life with a rosier hue—without the benefit of any artificial crutches or additives.

To Gloria's surprise, Christina put out her hand. "Fresh start?"

Tension drained out of her and for the first time since she'd entered the room, Gloria really smiled as she took the hand that was offered. "Fresh start."

Sierra placed her own hand on top of her sisters' clasped ones. She beamed as she looked from one to the other.

"Fresh start," she echoed.

And suddenly, just like that, it felt like old times. Gloria embraced the feeling just as she embraced the sisters she had been without for much too long. A huge sense of relief hovered like a cleansing cloud within the room.

The sisters all sank down onto the thickly padded brown leather sofa that dominated the room, shy, but eager to catch up and make up for lost time.

On the coffee table sat a bottle of wine and three glasses. Gloria ignored the alcohol and instead took a sip from the glass of seltzer she had brought with her. She thought about what had just been pledged. A fresh start. Something she intended to make a reality. "You know, for this to be a true fresh start, we have to give it all our attention."

"I'm for that." Christina poured Sierra a glass of wine, then one for herself. She hesitated over the third glass, then raised her eyes to Gloria.

Gloria smiled, then shook her head. Unlike their mother, her sisters were aware of her demons. At least, some of them.

"Don't worry about me." She indicated the glass of seltzer. "I'm fine with this."

"You've already made your fresh start," Christina observed, setting the bottle back on the tray.

"One day at a time." They raised their glasses and toasted a new beginning. Gloria caught her lower lip between her teeth as she regarded the other two thoughtfully. "You know what the single most disastrous obstacle in our path to recovery is?"

Sierra gamely placed her glass on the tray. "I'll bite, what?"

Gloria thought of her ill-fated marriage and the men who had come before. Christina had fared little better. As for Sierra, she had never found anyone to make her happy, either.

"Men," she told the others.

Christina laughed. "They are a problem, bless their black hearts."

"No," Gloria contradicted, "we're the problem." The other two women looked at her. "We can't seem to choose the right ones."

Sierra and Christina readily agreed with the assessment.

"That's because the rotten ones are always so damn attractive," Sierra observed.

Christina nodded. "Sure can't tell a book by its cover."

And the handsome ones knew they could get by on their looks and not take any responsibility for their actions. Well, she was swearing them off, the lot of them. And for the time being, so should her sisters. "So we're going to close the bookstore." But that sounded too final, so she added, "Temporarily."

Christina frowned. Leaning over, she pretended to look into the glass that Gloria was holding. "Sure that isn't vodka?" Rather than answer, Gloria held the glass out to her. Christina took it and sniffed. Bubbles were still dancing on top of the liquid. She wrinkled her nose as she pushed the glass back toward Gloria. "Seltzer," she confirmed.

Satisfied that she had her sisters' attention and compliance, Gloria continued. "We're not going to have anything to do with them."

Sierra shook her head. That seemed like rather an impossible resolution. "Pretty hard, considering they're almost half the population."

"On a private, social level," Gloria clarified. Her eyes shifted from Christina to Sierra to see if they were still with her. "Meaning, no dates."

"No dates," Sierra echoed. A beat later, she smiled, as if the words and their import were sinking in. "No dates," she repeated.

Christina held up her hand, taking a solemn oath. "No dates."

She couldn't tell if they were humoring her or if she'd really gotten through. "No, I'm serious," Gloria insisted. Warming up to her subject, she moved to the edge of the sofa, like a bird about to dive-bomb. "We shouldn't go out with any of them—no matter how tempted we are—" She stopped, deep in thought. "For a year," she concluded, then repeated, "A year. That should be long enough to at least begin to get the rest of our lives in order."

There was no one in her life, significant or otherwise. Sierra shrugged. There was nothing to lose. "Okay."

Christina laughed. It was obvious by her expression that the idea amused her. And maybe it had merit. "Fine by me."

They still weren't taking this seriously. She could tell.

Adamant, Gloria shook her head. "You say that now, but the first minute some cute, rotten guy crosses your path—"

"I'll ignore him," Christina concluded.

She had to up the ante, Gloria thought. Otherwise her sisters weren't going to give this the attention it needed. She firmly believed that men were the distracting force. Worse, they were the destructive force. If she and her sisters were going to accomplish anything with their lives, they had to remain focused.

"Right," Gloria said firmly. "And do you know why you'll ignore him?"

"Because I've finally gotten some sense in my head?" Christina guessed.

"No, because if you don't ignore him, you're going

to have to do something drastic in reparation, something you don't want to do."

"What wouldn't you want to do?" Sierra asked.

Thoughts flew through her brain in rapid-fire succession. "Put on a French maid's costume and clean up your apartments."

Christina's mouth fell open. "So if you fail, you'd be willing to fly in from Denver to—"

"Not from Denver," Gloria corrected. "From here."

Christina's look of surprise only intensified. "You've moved here?"

Gloria grinned. Since her mother had cut her off when she'd tried to share her news, her sisters were going to be the first to know. "In the process."

Christina's eyes widened. "You're kidding. Me, too." When the other two looked at her in stunned shock, she shrugged. "I got homesick for Papa's cooking." It was a handy enough excuse. Their father owned and operated Red, a restaurant whose patronage came from miles around just to sample the food.

"Okay, so it's agreed." Eager to get this on track and settled before the conversation could veer off again, Gloria held up her hand as if to take a solemn oath. "I promise to become a servant to each of you for the length of—" Again she paused before continuing. "One day each if I go back on our bargain." She looked at Sierra. "Your turn."

"Um…okay, I'll cook each of you a fantastic meal."

"You mean, you'll order take-out." Christina laughed.

"No, really, a great meal. From scratch," Sierra promised. "And you all know how I hate to cook."

"Sounds fair," Gloria commented. "Tina?"

Christina sighed, obviously trying to think. "Okay, I've got it. I'll wash cars for a whole day at the car wash. You can put up signs if you want. And I'll donate the money to charity. Satisfied?" she asked Gloria.

"Satisfied," Gloria announced, grinning. Then she looked from one sister to the other. "We all agreed?"

Christina shrugged her shoulders good-naturedly. "Sure, why not? Agreed." She took a sip of her wine to seal the bargain.

Sierra echoed the word, "Agreed," then took a sip herself. She grinned at Gloria. "Moving here, huh?"

The second the announcement had come out of her mouth, she'd known it had felt right. "Just as soon as I can find an apartment."

"Well, you're in luck," Sierra told her. The other two looked at her. "I know this really nice place. A friend of mine is relocating to the east coast. She's looking for someone to sublet the place. Interested?"

"You bet," Gloria enthused. And then she looked at her sisters again, a warm feeling spreading through her limbs. This was what she'd missed. What she needed.

Christina put it into words for her. "Wow, the Mendoza girls, back together again. Who would have thunk it?"

Gloria laughed, then turned and glanced toward the door. Crossing to it, she knocked loudly. "Hey, Mama, you can open the door now. We're friends again."

Christina came up to join her with Sierra bringing up the rear. "Think she can hear us?"

"She's a mother, of course she can hear us." As if to give credence to her words, the door flew open and Maria walked in, beaming at her daughters. "Especially when she's only two inches away," Gloria concluded.

They laughed and hugged, a human knot of arms and warmth, just like when they were small.

And at that moment, Gloria had never felt happier. She was home.

Chapter Two

Chapter Two

Jack Fortune walked out of the third-floor office and headed back toward the elevator. He punched the up button, which was already lit, impatience tap-dancing through him like the feet of a troop of dancers doing an Irish jig. He was not a happy man and his displeasure had nothing to do with his fighting off the lingering effects of jet lag that had attached themselves to him less than two hours ago when he'd made the flight in from New York's JFK.

It was what lay waiting for him in the immediate future that bothered Jack.

He seldom resented doing practically anything his father asked of him. He had more than a healthy respect for Patrick Fortune, both as a businessman and as a human being. If children were allowed to preselect their father, he knew that he sure as hell couldn't have asked for better than the one he had. He would have done anything in the world for his father without hesitation.

But this wasn't for his father—not really. No. He had been pulled away from his enormously busy schedule at the New York office of Fortune-Rockwell Bank to help out some friend of his father's daughter set up shop in San Antonio. The whole thing had sounded rather slapdash when Patrick had called him about it the day before yesterday, asking him to fly out to lend his business acumen to this so-called enterprise.

Jack punched the button again, frowning. This was undoubtedly some bubbleheaded female who thought just because she had a whim, she could make a go of a business. Probably didn't even know the first thing that was involved in such an undertaking.

Jewelry-making, for God's sake. What was his father thinking? The woman had probably gotten some kit from a craft store for Christmas and thought she was going to take the market by storm because she could string together ten beads or whatever.

He'd dearly wanted to say as much when his father had called to drop this little bomb in his lap, but he'd held his tongue out of respect and out of love.

Jack shifted his six-foot-two-inch frame. Where the hell was the elevator, anyway?

Damn, his father should know better, he thought.

Hadn't he told him more than once that he was a vital member of the Fortune-Rockwell team? If he was so vital, then he should remain in the New York office, not have to come gallivanting out to San Antonio to hold some novice's well-manicured hand.

Once upon a time, his father would have known that. But lately, Jack thought, concern nibbling away at him, his father was showing signs of slowing down. Whenever they spoke, Patrick Fortune would talk about "smelling the roses" and all that stuff people who've had a near-death experience say. Except that, at seventy, his father seemed as strong as ever. And when he'd asked him if there was something wrong, if he was perhaps not feeling well, his father had heartily said no, laughing at the very notion. Patrick Fortune had said that for the first time in his life, there was nothing wrong. That he'd finally had the good fortune—no pun intended— of seeing life the right way.

It seemed to Jack a case of too much denial. The more he thought about it now, the more convinced he became that there was something wrong with his father. The dynamo who had helped build up and was now in charge of Fortune-Rockwell Bank didn't stop to smell roses he could have delivered to him, nor did he take key personnel and ship them off to San Antonio because some chicklet's mother asked him to.

From what he'd gathered, not only had his father agreed to help get this Gloria Mendoza Something-or-Other's business up and running, but he'd taken on her sister, Christina, as well. He'd put her to work in the San Antonio branch as a business analyst for his best friend, Derek Rockwell, the Rockwell behind the second half of the bank's name.

Something was definitely up.

Maybe his father was going through his second childhood. After all, the man was living in his seventh decade and, despite power, prestige and a loving family, maybe Patrick Fortune thought that he had missed out on something the first time around.

It was time Jack had a long talk with his father. Later. Right now, he'd promised to meet with his father and this Gloria person.

He punched the up button a third time. If his father's office wasn't on the thirtieth floor, he would have given up and walked up. Served him right for stopping off to see if one of his old acquaintances was still with the company. Business before pleasure. He could have always caught up with his friend after he'd put in an appearance at his dad's office.

Maybe if he could get his father to see just how ridiculous it was to ask him to get involved in this, the senior Fortune would let him go back to New York where he belonged instead of making him cool his heels in San Antonio. God knew he had better things to do than act as a guardian angel for an empty-headed female.

After all, his father had already brought Derek out here. Why have both his right-hand and left-hand man in the same place?

The elevator doors opened in front of him. Finally!

Immersed in his own thoughts, searching for a way out of his dilemma, Jack stepped into the car.

There were several other people in the car, including one woman who blocked the keypad. To press his floor button, he would have to move her out of the way.

He had no time for games and was in no mood for them. "Thirty," he snapped when the woman made no effort to step back.

Gloria was busy struggling with a bout of claustrophobia, a battle she was forced to engage in every time she stepped onto an elevator. The fact that there were several people in the car only made things worse. Dazed, she looked at the man who'd gotten on. Until he'd opened his mouth, she'd thought he was quite an attention-getter. She sincerely doubted that she'd ever seen a man as good-looking as this one off a movie screen.

But the second he opened his mouth, attitude came pouring out. Attitude she was in no mood for. Besides the claustrophobia, she was nervous. It wasn't every day of the year that Patrick Fortune offered to back you and help you get on your feet financially.

Not that she needed it as much as her mother seemed to think. She'd packed up her business in Denver and left with everything in good standing. She was more than comfortably in the black, with a number of back orders left to fill. Even at this early date, it looked as if the year was shaping up nicely for her.

She had every confidence in the world that she was going to succeed here, as well. But it never hurt to be given an added boost—and by Patrick Fortune, no less. He'd seemed like such a nice man when she'd talked to him at the party. He'd even admired the necklace she'd been wearing, an original piece she'd made for herself.

But that had been pleasure and this was business. So there were butterflies roaming around in her stomach.

She slanted a look at the rude man. He hadn't even said please.

"I'm not the elevator operator," she informed him crisply.

She saw his dark eyes narrow and he looked like Zeus about to hurl thunderbolts from Mount Olympus. "If you don't want the job, then don't stand in front of the keypad."

She was not about to be bullied. She'd paid her dues in that department and no man was ever going to order her around again. Arms spread out on either side of her, she took a step back, leaving the way clear for him to press the keypad himself.

"You know, nice people get a lot further in this world than people with bad attitudes."

"You tell 'im, honey," someone in the back of the elevator encouraged.

"And people who mind their own business get further," the rude man retorted.

* * *

Annoyed, Jack glanced to see which floor they'd just passed, then pressed the very next number. The last thing he needed was to ride up to his destination sharing the experience with a harpy.

This was shaping up to be a bad morning all around, Jack silently conceded. They'd lost his luggage at the airport, the limousine that was to have met him never showed up and the taxi he'd wound up taking had gotten stuck in traffic. Even if he had been in the best of moods, his patience would have been severely challenged.

His natural inclination to be polite was strained and had completely fallen by the wayside the second the woman hovering over the elevator keypad had given him a flippant answer to his request.

The elevator stopped on his floor and opened its doors. Jack was out like a shot.

Gloria heard herself breathe a sigh of relief.

Now *there* was a serial killer in the making, she thought, glad he'd gotten off. At the very least, it was one less body to deal with.

The doors closed again. She pressed damp hands together, afraid of leaving a mark on the wintergreen suit she was wearing. She felt a hitch in her throat and told herself she was just nervous.

Nothing to be nervous about. Patrick Fortune's a nice man.

After all, she and Patrick Fortune had gotten along

famously at the party. Within a few minutes of speaking with him, Gloria felt as if she'd known him all of her life.

He'd been attentive and interested in everything she'd had to say about her business, giving her the same kind of courtesy he would a captain of industry. Her mother had told her later that he was seventy, but he certainly hadn't acted it or looked it. Athletic, five-ten, with mostly red hair, he'd been charming and infinitely reassuring. After talking to him, she'd known that bringing her business to San Antonio was going to be a lot easier than she'd thought. He'd even proposed backing a loan for whatever she'd needed.

Their encounter had been reassuring. There was no reason in the world to be nervous. And yet, she was.

It had been a good thing, coming home, she decided, shifting to the side as she allowed three people to get off, grateful for their departure.

Now that she had returned, she didn't know why she'd hesitated for so long. Instead of everything falling apart, the way she'd once thought, things were finally coming together. Maybe it had taken her leaving home to make her appreciate everything she actually did have, she mused as the climb to the thirtieth floor continued.

Whatever it was, she was glad she'd heeded her mother's call to come home when she had instead of deliberating a few more days. Otherwise she wouldn't have gotten to meet Patrick Fortune.

But then again, she mused, a smile curving her

mouth, knowing her mother, she probably would have run into the man sooner or later. Maria Mendoza didn't leave much to chance if she could help it.

She'd do well to take a page out of her mother's book, Gloria decided.

The elevator finally came to a stop on the thirtieth floor. Gloria was alone in the car. She stepped through the steel doors, taking a deep breath as she did so, relieved to be out of the box.

And then she took in her surroundings.

She felt a little like a mortal reaching Mount Olympus, seeking an audience with Zeus.

As she walked to the receptionist's desk, she again thought about the man she'd met the other night. She'd found Patrick Fortune extremely easy to talk to. Like a kindly uncle. She would have expected him to be driven, anal, like that man who'd just scowled at her in the elevator.

Her thoughts going there, she pitied anyone having to deal with that one. The next moment, she put him out of her mind.

The walls that led to the receptionist's desk were lined with paintings—bright, colorful landscapes and seascapes that were extremely uplifting. Just looking at them made her feel empowered.

She wondered if Patrick Fortune had selected them himself. Probably. He didn't strike her as a man who delegated very much.

Reaching the long, ivory-colored desk, Gloria smiled

and nodded at the receptionist. "I'm Gloria Mendoza Johansen. I have an appointment to see Mr. Fortune."

The woman behind the desk flashed her a studied smile that disappeared a moment after making its appearance. Her small, stubby fingers flew over her keyboard with the flair of a piano virtuoso playing a well-beloved concerto.

"Yes," the woman whose nameplate proclaimed her to be Doris Wells verified in a thick Texas accent, "it looks like you do."

Before she could reach for her telephone to notify her boss about this newest arrival, the door behind her opened. Patrick Fortune, wearing an iron-gray suit and light salmon shirt with a gray tie stepped out. He smiled warmly at her as he stepped forward.

"Gloria, right on time." He glanced at his watch. "A few minutes early, as a matter of fact. I like that in a person. Always get there one jump ahead." He took both of her hands in his. "You look lovely."

And then, as if aware that he was suddenly a source of interest, he glanced toward the receptionist. The woman had raised her brow at the friendly display.

"Stop frowning like that, Doris. I'm not putting the moves on Ms. Johansen, I'm just making a very obvious observation. Besides, I'm old enough to be her gr—" He cleared his throat and amended, "Father." A twinkle came into his eye as he tucked Gloria's arm through his and led her toward his office. "Come in, come in."

His office took her breath away. She was vaguely aware that he'd left the door open, as if to leave a connection with reality.

Patrick Fortune inclined his head, conceding, "It's a little large."

A little large? Obviously the man had a gift for understatement. Her observation came out in an awed whisper. "I've seen smaller golf courses."

Her words were rewarded with a deep, booming laugh.

"Your mother warned me that you always say what you think."

She flushed, wondering if she'd offended him somehow, or shown him the small, frightened girl who lived behind the larger-than-life dream and words.

"My mother always told me to think of what I say before I say it."

That had been the source of more than one lecture she'd been forced to endure. Always her own person even when she didn't know who or what that person might be, Gloria had always felt driven to do her own thing, not to try to conform to anyone else's image of her. Now, she realized that her image of herself was what her mother had had in mind all along.

Another sign that her homecoming was a good thing. She took heart in that.

"Your mother is a lovely woman. I've known her and your father for almost as long as I've known Rosita and Rueben Perez." Her parents' best friends, Gloria thought, not to mention that Rosita and her mother were cousins, as well. Rosita had worked for the Fortunes, taking care of their children, since what felt like the beginning of time. She supposed, in part, she had the other woman to thank for this opportunity, as well.

Maybe, Gloria mused, she was finally due for some honest-to-goodness good luck.

Rather than resist the way she would have even five years ago, insisting that her mother was meddling, she now gladly left herself open to "be meddled with." Heaven knew that no one could do a worse job than she had with her life up to two years ago.

Maybe, if she'd left herself open to suggestions earlier instead of resisting them, her life would have laid itself out differently. Better.

This wasn't the time for reflections, much less regrets, she admonished herself. The past was just that, something to remain in the background. She was here to take advantage of the present and to hopefully, finally, build a very solid future.

This was the new, improved Gloria whose roots were firmly entrenched in the Gloria who had once been, before the drugs and alcohol had interfered with the direction her life was taking.

She offered the older man her best smile, the one her mother claimed lit up her whole face. "She speaks very highly of you, Mr. Fortune. Both my parents do."

He gestured her toward the chair that was in front of his desk and waited until she sat before he took his own seat. "And they speak highly of you."

She knew how much heartache she'd caused both her parents. Their loyalty took her breath away. And made her ashamed all over again for what she had done to them. "They do?"

Patrick had five children himself, just like the Mendozas, and he could well guess what she was thinking. Maria hadn't gone into detail, but he knew there was a black period in Gloria's past.

She was about Violet's age, he judged. "Just because our children temporarily 'mess up,' doesn't mean that we suddenly are blind to their good points. Sometimes, that's all we parents have to hold on to while we ride out the turbulence."

She smiled ruefully and shook her head, rising to her feet. "I can't imagine any of your children giving you a problem."

He laughed, the sound echoing within the large room. "Then I fear that you have far less imagination than I have been given to believe you possess." He winked at her.

Which was exactly when his son walked in.

Jack stopped just half a step past the threshold, stunned. His father had just winked at what appeared, at least from the back, to be an attractive woman.

She was wearing a trim-fitting jacket and short skirt, the latter of which hugged hips the way, he judged, most men of her acquaintance probably would have wanted to. Her head came up to his father's shoulder.

Since the man was about five-ten, that placed her in the neighborhood of petite. She had deep-black hair that was pinned up. Even so, she didn't appear to be here on business, not if that wink he'd just witnessed was any indication of what was transpiring.

He'd obviously interrupted something, but his father had told him to be here at this time, so here he was.

Jack couldn't help wondering if this was the reason for his father's change in attitude over the past few months. Was he advocating smelling roses because there was now a mistress to receive those roses?

For a second Jack debated stepping out again. But his father looked in his direction.

"So, you've finally gotten here." The greeting was accompanied by a wide smile.

His father didn't look like a man who'd just been caught in a transgression. But then, Patrick Fortune was the most self-assured man he had ever met. To his recollection, his father had never made any apologies for himself or his actions.

Aware that he was actually a few minutes late, something he abhorred, Jack found himself on the defensive. "I, um, had to catch another elevator car. There was this obnoxious woman—"

The rest of his statement faded into the light blue walls. The woman his father had just winked at turned around and looked at him.

A feeling of déjà vu shot through him with the velocity of an iron-tipped arrow.

He hadn't recognized the woman's clothes, or even the color of her hair, but then she turned to look at him and, well, that wasn't the kind of face a man easily forgot.

Not even if he tried.

Gloria stared at the man framed in the doorway, recognizing him instantly. It was the man who'd been so rude he'd managed to bring out the worst in her at an incredibly fast speed. Mr. Fortune obviously knew him. More than that, he seemed to have been waiting for him.

Why? What did this mean?

Suddenly there was a distinct sinking sensation in the pit of her stomach. Her fingertips felt moist again, the way they always did when she felt the walls closing in around her.

Was it a premonition?

Holding her breath, Gloria turned away from the younger man in the doorway and looked at Patrick Fortune, a silent, formless prayer echoing in her brain.

Patrick's eyes shifted from his son to the woman in front of him and back again. He had gotten to his present station in life through hard work coupled with very keen instinct. Instinct that was at times sharper than others', but even at its worst was never dull.

Right now his instincts told him that there was something going on here between Maria's daughter and his son that he wasn't quite aware of. Something he might be able to capitalize on.

He adopted an innocent expression as he looked from one to the other again. "You two know each other?"

"No." Gloria shot the word out like a bullet.

Jack, Patrick noted, hadn't taken his eyes off Gloria since he walked in. "We rode up together in the elevator." The words were ground out.

A slightly puzzled note entered into his expression. "If you rode up together, then why—"

Anticipation had Gloria interrupting. "He got off early," she supplied.

Jack set his jaw hard. Not adding, as he wanted to, that he'd gotten off because he hadn't felt like riding up all those floors with an obvious shrew.

This *couldn't* be the woman his father wanted him to work with, Jack thought. His luck didn't run that bad.

Chapter Three

His father was looking at him, obviously still waiting for some kind of good, believable explanation as to why he'd gotten off on another floor rather than arrive here with this annoying woman.

Jack was sharp when it came to matters in the boardroom. But personal things, such as his reaction to this woman, were another matter. The only excuse he could come up with was, "I forgot something."

Patrick nodded, wise enough to let the matter drop. Jack doubted that his father really believed him, but was clearly willing to let it go. For now.

"Nothing important, I trust," Patrick said, eyeing his firstborn.

"Excuse me?"

"That 'thing' you forgot, it was nothing important, I trust," Patrick repeated. Just the slightest hint of humor curved his mouth as he continued to look at Jack.

"No, nothing important," Jack murmured. *Just my sanity.*

Patrick's eyes never left his son's face. Jack was so much a chip off the old block that at times it was positively scary. He saw himself in Jack's eyes, in Jack's actions. Which was why, when Maria Mendoza had approached him for help regarding her daughters, the first thing he'd thought of was to get Jack involved in Gloria's business transfer. He knew that, given Jack's business acumen, it was a little like offering a building contractor a set of rubber blocks. But he wasn't necessarily looking to challenge Jack. Not professionally, at any rate. The challenge he offered was to the inner man, the one whose development had been arrested all these years. Ever since Jack's college days.

It was high time that Jack stop playing the one note he was so exceptionally skilled at playing and fill out the other corners of his life.

Patrick was aware, although Jack never spoke about it, that his son had had his heart set on marrying Ann Garrison, a girl he'd known in college. When she was killed while driving under the influence one night, nearly taking Jack with her, his oldest had withdrawn from the world. But then slowly, with the support of his family, Jack had crawled back out and thrown himself into the family business.

In the beginning he'd been very grateful that Jack had found a way to help himself heal. But after a while, it had become apparent that this was the only path his son would take.

Nothing mattered but the banking business and that was wrong. He'd learned that the hard way himself. It was a lesson he meant to pass on to Jack even if Jack resisted. He didn't want his son looking back at the end of his years and seeing nothing but cold accomplishments to have marked his passage through this earth.

A man needed a family. His own family. And children. Gloria might not be the one Jack ultimately wound up with, but considering the fact that his son wasn't out looking at all, Gloria seemed more than capable of getting him interested in pursuits other than business.

Patrick had a knack for reading people and Gloria didn't look the type to be intimidated. At the very least, he doubted if his slightly larger-than-life son would plow the woman under. She could probably go ten rounds with Jack and still hold her own.

And if he read between the lines of what Maria had told him about her daughter, Gloria could use the stimulation, as well.

Right now, though, silence was hanging extremely heavily in the room. Patrick felt as if he was the impromptu referee at an unofficial bout.

Mentally he rubbed his hands together. *Let the games begin,* he thought.

"Well, then, let's get on with it. I suppose formal introductions are in order. Jack, I'd like you to meet your, um, new 'project.'" Patrick flashed a smile at the young woman. "Gloria Mendoza Johansen. Gloria, this is my oldest son, Jack." He didn't bother hiding the pride in his voice. Life was too short to scrimp on praise when it was due. "Next to me, I'd say that Jack is the most savvy businessman I know. He'll be handling your affairs." His smile widened. "So to speak."

She'd never seen eyes that twinkled before. But there was definitely a twinkle in Patrick Fortune's eyes. Why?

And his words caused alarms to go off in her head. "You mean that you're not going to be overseeing the shop?" She'd thought that was why he'd asked her here. But he was palming her off on his son, Mr. Charm-and-Personality.

It was the last thing she wanted. Recovering from the jolt, her first instinct was to say, "Thanks, but no thanks." After all, she'd originally started the business in Denver all by herself and it had been doing very nicely, thank you very much. Over the two years that it had been in existence, the store had gained a small but loyal and solid following. And she had contractual work in Hollywood, as well. An actress on a popular sitcom had fallen in love with one of her necklace designs and suddenly she was getting calls from the west coast, asking her to create the jewelry for the whole show.

All of this had come about on the strength of her skill and by word of mouth. There was even a man in New York City who'd flown out to buy his wife a Christmas present. His wife had seen her work while vacationing in Denver and had fallen in love with it. And he knew some people who knew some people... Whatever it took to build up a clientele, she mused.

There was absolutely no reason why she couldn't do that right here in San Antonio. After all, this was only a stone's throw from where she'd originally started out, Red Rock. She already knew people here.

But there was no denying that the Fortunes were a power to be reckoned with and when one of them offered to show up in your corner, you didn't suddenly throw up a brick wall to keep them out. Especially not the head of the clan.

But this is the son, not the father. A scowling son at that, she reminded herself.

There were times when Gloria was certain that fate had it in for her. One moment it looked as if things were only going to get better, the next, the rug beneath her feet was being frantically tugged on. As of yet, it hadn't been pulled out, but it did provide just enough turbulence to throw her off balance.

She didn't like being off balance. She'd spent enough of her life that way already.

Patrick's expression was disarming. It left no room for argument.

"I'm afraid I'm going to be too busy to offer you the personal attention that you deserve." He let his words sink in properly, then looked at Jack.

Oh, and I won't be? Jack thought. His father had never minimized his contribution to the business or his importance in the company before. Just what was going on here?

"Would you excuse us for a second?" Jack said, addressing Gloria.

"Sure," Gloria replied, and left the room.

Moving over toward the full-length bar that had been the last piece of decor installed in his more-than-spacious, state-of-the-art office, Patrick Fortune waited for Jack to begin.

Jack turned his back to the door to further ensure their privacy. "Dad, have I done something to displease you?"

"On the contrary, I couldn't have asked for a better right hand—or a better son," Patrick answered.

Okay, so he hadn't unconsciously incurred his father's annoyance, Jack thought. His mind did a U-turn. Did Derek have something to do with this? Derek Rockwell had been his best friend for years now. Jack had been the one to initially bring Derek to his father's attention, feeling sorry for Derek because he had never experienced the kind of warm family interactions that existed within his own home. Derek's scholastic path had shadowed Jack's and when the time came, his father had taken him into the company with open arms. More than that, his father had all but adopted Derek, treating him more like a son than Derek's own father ever had.

Had Derek managed to somehow usurp him?

No, that was a low, petty thought. Derek would never turn on him, never do things behind his back. The man was selfless. Besides, his father had asked Derek to come to the San Antonio office weeks before he'd sent for him, Jack thought.

Jack stopped speculating. "Then why am I playing nursemaid to this woman?"

Patrick shook his head, his expression a portrait of patience. "Not nursemaid, I assure you. And it's only temporary. Look, this is a favor for a friend," he repeated, "and I would appreciate it if you would give this venture your very best effort."

Jack blew out a breath. "I can do what's required in my sleep," he protested.

The indulgent smile returned to his father's lips. "I'd prefer you awake."

There just had to be more to this than met the eye. "Dad—"

Patrick placed his hand on Jack's shoulder, the simple action calling a halt to any and all further protest. "How many times have I asked you to do me a favor?"

For a moment the wind left Jack's sails. His father never presumed to manipulate him. The man had trusted his judgment and, except for a few initial guidelines, had given him free rein when it came to running the New York office.

Jack measured out his words. "This would be the first."

"Right, it would be. So you know that this is important to me." And Jack could tell that it was.

Jack glanced at the woman standing just outside the door. *Why* was this so important to his father? And then an answer occurred to him. One he didn't particularly like. He looked at his father for a long moment. "Dad, is there more going on here than you're telling me?"

Patrick's reddish eyebrows huddled together over the bridge of his nose. "More?"

Suddenly his giant reservoir of words was mostly empty. "You know, is she…are the two of you—"

Because he thought so highly of his father—and *always* had—Jack couldn't bring himself to finish the sentence. Did Gloria represent his father's lost youth?

Patrick was staring at him with a look of incredulity. When he spoke, his voice was hardly louder than a whisper. "Are you actually asking me if I'm having an affair with her?"

He'd seen his father become angry once or twice, although never with him or anyone in the family. He wasn't sure what he was about to witness now. Jack held his ground. Because if his father was having an affair, he was damn well going to talk him out of it. And get rid of the girl as quickly as was humanly possible without involving something with a firing pin.

His eyes never left his father's. "Yes."

For a second Patrick stood stock-still. Then he scrubbed his hand over his face, his expression still stunned. "My God, I don't know whether to be flattered or angry." He laughed and Jack knew that the danger had passed. "My boy, your mother, God bless her, is more than enough woman for me."

"Well, if you're not having an affair with her and you're not annoyed with me, why are you asking me to do this?"

The answer was simple. "Because she needs help." *And because you do, too,* Patrick added silently. "She's had a rough time of it."

"Rough time?"

"You know, personally." Patrick's words came out at a faster clip, as if he was running short on time. "It's too complicated to talk about now, but I thought that you of all people might be sympathetic." He then issued the only instructions he was about to give on the matter. "Help her get on her feet. Not be taken advantage of, that sort of thing." And then, apparently because he didn't want Jack to think that he was dealing with someone lacking in business sense, he added, "Don't get me wrong—Gloria's savvy. But two heads are always better than one."

"Unless they belong to the same person," Jack muttered under his breath, hating this corner he was being painted into.

About to walk back to Gloria, Patrick stopped and turned around to look at Jack. "What?"

Jack waved away his words. He might as well make the best of this. The sooner he got down to it, the sooner he'd be finished. "Okay. I'll do it."

"Knew you would," Patrick said, moving toward the door.

Reaching Gloria, Patrick beamed and led her back into the office. Then he glanced at his watch. "I'm afraid I'm running a little behind."

"Meeting?" Jack asked, instantly alert.

"In a matter of speaking." Patrick's expression softened slightly. "Telephone conferencing."

Apparently hoping for a last-minute reprieve or, at the very least, a stay of execution while he was included in this conference, Jack was quick to ask, "Is it anyone that I know?"

"Intimately." The word hung in the air between them for a second before Patrick added, "I promised to call your mother." His eyes shifted to Gloria. "I have to run, Gloria, but I'm leaving you in very capable hands."

From the look in Jack Fortune's eyes as he turned toward her, Gloria had more than a passing suspicion that he wanted to use those very capable hands to wring her neck.

Unconsciously she squared her shoulders, standing almost at attention by the time he reached her. The closer he got, the more tension telegraphed itself through her body.

And the closer he got, the handsomer he looked.

There was no doubt about it, she thought, attempting to remain impartial in her judgment, Jack Fortune was one of those men that the term "drop-dead gorgeous" had been invented to describe.

The kind of man she might have once fallen for before introductions were even completed.

Lucky for her she'd done a great deal of growing and changing since those days. Lucky, too, that he'd managed to put her off so completely with the very first words that had come out of his mouth. If anything, it had been a matter of annoyance at first glance.

And if there was one thing she was utterly sure of, it was that Mr. Jack Fortune posed no threat to her state of mind or the pact she had made with her sisters. If for some reason her hormones decided to go berserk and she was tempted to renege on that pact, it wasn't about to be with a man who used his tongue as a carving knife at Thanksgiving.

For one thing, she'd seen warmer eyes on a mackerel lying on display at the fish market than the ones that were turned on her now.

She was acutely aware that they were being left alone in this cavern of an office suite. Patrick Fortune waved to her as he took out his cell phone and slipped away into a private alcove where he could rendezvous with his wife of more than forty years.

Must be nice, she thought, to love someone that much, to want to remain married to them for so many years. Like her parents. Too bad it was never going to happen to her.

But she had her business to keep her busy, she reminded herself. And so it was time to get back to that business.

She looked at Jack. "You're not happy about this, are you?"

"Whether I'm happy has nothing to do with this," he told her coldly, eyeing the purse she had tucked under her arm. It was one of those flimsy clutch things big enough for a change purse, a driver's license and a set of keys. She obviously hadn't brought any papers with her that he could look over. It figured.

"Since you don't seem to have anything with you, why don't we make an appointment for another time?"

She looked at him blankly. Maybe he should be speaking in monosyllabic words.

"Sometime when you have something with you for me to look over."

"'Something'?"

He took a breath, then spelled it out for her. Slowly. "Blueprints for the space you'll need. Inventory of the items you'll need on hand. Everything from shipping boxes to Bunsen burners. Cash-flow projections," he added for good measure, wondering if she was following him at all.

"I don't use a Bunsen burner," she informed him tersely.

Jack looked down at her, then found himself caught

in the fire in her eyes. He was about to say something else when he suddenly became aware that her very trim figure was just inches away from him and that something quite apart from a business meeting was going on here. It was as if all the pores in his body had suddenly opened up and were inhaling her very feminine, very unsettling perfume.

The woman was female with a capital "F."

The very last thing he wanted in his life.

With effort, he steered himself back to his indignation. "Do you even have any idea what it takes to set up a business?"

She bit her lower lip. "I—"

He made himself look at her eyes instead of her mouth. Like a man sitting in the middle of a boat that had suddenly broken apart, he felt compelled to clutch at something for survival. In this case, he needed to drive her away. "Did anyone tell you that most businesses fail in their first year?"

She hated his high-handed tone and it took effort for her not to turn on her heel and just walk out.

She could feel her nails digging into her palms as she struggled to rein in the temper she had inherited from her mother. This pompous ass was actually talking down to her, treating her as if she was some kind of a kindergarten dropout. Just because his last name was Fortune didn't give him the right to act as if she was some kind of mental incompetent.

Because she owed it to Patrick not to kill his son, she

forced a smile to her lips. "Then I guess we have nothing to worry about."

"Meaning?" Jack demanded, the word scratching his throat as it climbed out. Jack felt like a man who was losing his mind. Part of him wanted to walk out and slam the door on this woman. And another part of him wanted to find out what full lips with a slash of pink lipstick tasted like.

"Meaning this isn't my first year."

Flipping open her purse, she took out a folded magazine article. Very precisely she unfolded it, then handed it to him.

"I've been in business for two years now. My store was located in Denver." She took the article—clipped from a local Denver Sunday supplement; a story featuring her unique designs—out of his hand, noting that he hadn't even glanced at it. He kept his eyes on her. "I'm not a virgin, Mr. Fortune."

Chapter Four

It took Jack longer than he would have liked to pull himself together. "Bragging, Ms. Johansen?"

Gloria raised her chin, a bantam rooster unafraid of the fox.

"It's *Mrs.* Johansen—or it was." She was seriously thinking of changing her name back to simply Mendoza but for now she kept that to herself. "But since we're going to be working together, I think you should call me Gloria, *Jack.*" She looked him in the eye as she deliberately emphasized his name. "And what I'm saying—" God, it was hard to talk to this man without clenching her teeth and pushing the words out "—is that I had a good business going in Denver."

"Then why move?"

If there was one thing that got the hairs on the back of her neck to stand up straight, it was having to explain herself. She'd resisted the truth when the questions had come from her parents and she liked them a whole lot better than she did this intrusive man.

But she needed this boost. The Fortune backing meant a great deal in these parts and she was not about to turn her back on that just because Patrick Fortune had had the distinct *mis*fortune of siring one very mean-spirited son of a gun.

Telling herself that pride went before the fall, Gloria forced her lips into a wide, beatific smile. "Because this is home and I decided it was time to come home." And then, because she hated being on the hot seat, she turned the tables and asked him a question.

"Where's home for you?"

He'd been unprepared for her prying. And there was no way he was about to discuss anything private with a complete stranger. "That doesn't matter."

To which she responded by widening her smile. He could feel it slipping in under his skin. Warming him. But whether that was due to annoyance or just a man-woman thing, he couldn't tell.

"Home always matters," she told him in a voice that was far too sultry for the message it delivered.

Jack fought the effects the only way he knew how: with a sarcastic remark he knew would put her off.

"That sounds like something you'd find embroidered on a kitchen towel."

Undaunted, her smile never waned. "The kitchen's usually the heart of a home, especially in my house when I was growing up."

She kept throwing him curves. Did the woman suffer from Attention Deficit Disorder? "Just what does any of this have to do with business?"

This time he noticed that her smile did frost over just a little. "I'd thought you might want to know a little about the person whose business you're dipping your fingers into."

Jack frowned. She made it sound as if he was deliberately invading her. As if he even had any interest in such a small venture. She could just take herself to one of their branch offices and arrange for a loan if that was what this was all going to boil down to.

"There's no 'dipping,'" he informed her tersely, "there'll just be straightening."

Temper. Remember to keep your temper, Gloria cautioned herself. There wasn't anything to be gained by giving this man a piece of her mind. If she did, she knew her mother would get wind of it and probably think she'd gone back to her old ways. She wasn't about to add to the woman's concerns. No, she was going to be a lady about this if it killed her.

"There won't be much of that, either." Her voice was soft, melodious. "My business isn't in chaos, Jack, it just needs a loving hand to oversee it being unwrapped in San Antonio."

Her words produced startling images in his brain. Suddenly he saw himself sitting by a warm fireplace in some secluded little hideaway, removing the layers of her clothing one by one.

Was that just an acquired tan or was that the true hue of her skin?

Stunned, Jack pulled back.

What the hell was going on here? He didn't care if her tan was painted on, it made no difference to him. What was he doing, thinking like that?

He jumped on the words she'd used. "This isn't a love affair, it's a business—"

"It's both," she corrected before he could continue.

She obviously couldn't have lost him more if she'd thrown him headlong into the center of a cattle stampede and then ridden off, leaving him to be trampled.

"That's actually the name, you know."

"The name of what?"

"My jewelry store." What did he think she was talking about? Obviously the man wasn't as sharp as his father thought he was. "It's called 'Love Affair.'" She enunciated slowly for his benefit. His face looked like a road map to confusion. "Because that's what all my designs center around."

"A love affair," he repeated incredulously.

"With the skin." Even as she emphasized the concept, she could see that he wasn't following her. Not a dreamer, this one. What a surprise. She tried again, repeating her philosophy for him and speaking very slowly.

"The jewelry I design is supposed to be a love affair with the skin it touches, with the woman who owns the piece."

She could see that she wasn't getting through to him. Definitely not a sensitive man. She blew out a breath, unconsciously propping a fisted hand on her waist. "Work with me here."

He laughed dryly. The sound left her cold. "I don't seem to have a choice."

She cocked her head, doing an instant analysis. From where she was standing, it wasn't hard to read between the lines. His father was making him do this. "You don't strike me as someone who resigns himself to not having choices."

Was she trying to flatter him? Or pretending to be intuitive? He couldn't tell and it annoyed him not to be able to read her.

He decided to put her off for the time being, until he regrouped. "Look, as I said earlier, this would be much more productive if we rescheduled. Frankly, I just got off the plane and I'm not at my best."

"You have a gift for understatement I see." She couldn't help it. The words had broken free of their own accord. He'd handed her just too perfect a straight line. She flushed. "I mean—"

"Yes." He cut her off, trying not to notice that the

soft-pink hue of lipstick gave her an alluring look. "I know exactly what you mean." Since she was his only assignment while he was here in San Antonio, his schedule was pretty much open. Still, he did want to catch up with Derek while he was here and to see a few people who'd been out in the New York office until recently. "How does the day after tomorrow sound? Say around nine?"

She was happy to learn that he liked getting an early start. So did she. At least they had one thing in common. "That sounds fine to me." Since he hadn't mentioned location, she asked, "Where would you like to meet?"

At her new shop would be the perfect place, but it occurred to him that he didn't know if she had even selected a location yet or if she was still scouting them out. "Have you given any thought to where the shop is going to be?"

There he went again, treating her as if she had a brain the size of a pea. "As a matter of fact, I have. And it's perfect."

He'd be the judge of that, Jack thought. "All right, I'll come by and pick you up at your place and then we can take a look at this so-called perfect place."

She was in purgatory, Gloria thought, and doing penance for all the past sins of her life. But that was all right, she could get through this, she told herself. *That which doesn't kill us makes us stronger,* she recalled. And at this rate, she was going to be one hell of a strong woman.

"Fine." Taking a small pad out of her purse, she wrote down the necessary information for him. She tore off the page and handed it to Jack, tucking the pad back into her purse. "Here's the address."

"Fine," Jack murmured as he pocketed the slip of paper.

"Fine," she echoed. But it was definitely not fine in her book and wouldn't be fine until she had this man and the stick he had swallowed removed from her life. "Until then," she said prophetically, then walked out of the office.

Gloria lengthened her stride considerably once she was out of the office. Hurrying past Doris at the receptionist's desk she had the presence of mind to offer the woman a quick, perfunctory smile. Gloria didn't slow down until she reached the elevator. She couldn't wait to get away.

Entering the elevator, she felt the air immediately hitch in her throat.

What a jerk, she thought angrily. What a damn pompous jerk.

Trying to rein in the anger that was spiking through her, she punched the button for Christina's floor. She did *not* want to deal with Jack Fortune. She stared at the numbers as she descended.

Gloria caught her lower lip between her teeth, thinking. Maybe she'd ask her mother to speak to Patrick. There was no question that she'd rather deal with the senior Fortune than his stuck-up sarcastic snob of a son. The two men were as different as night and day.

And then she frowned.

She wasn't nine and involved in some scrap in the schoolyard. She was thirty years old, for God's sake, and had been around the proverbial block a few times. More than a few. Even at nine, she hadn't gone running to her mother for help. She'd always settled her own fights.

Nothing should have changed. She could handle the holier-than-thou Mr. Jack Fortune and she could do it with aplomb.

She calmed down as the idea of putting him in his place began to take hold. The man would never know what hit him, she promised herself. She'd gotten through rehab, a rotten marriage and dealt with an entire boatload of guilt and remorse along the way. Compared to that, dealing with Jack Fortune should be an absolute snap.

To underscore the thought, she snapped her fingers just as the elevator door opened. Right on time.

She grinned as she stepped out.

Christina held her questions in check until they were seated at the restaurant she'd selected; a fashionable one located on the tenth floor of the Fortune-Rockwell Bank building. Far from an employee cafeteria, it had earned a reputation for both its food and its affordable prices. Ever the practical one, her older sister had judged that although they both seemed to be on their way to bigger things, they could do with watching their money for a while.

She leaned forward across the small table for two and asked in a hushed whisper, "So? How did it go?"

Gloria took her lead from her older sister and leaned in toward her. "Awful."

Disappointment registered across Christina's face. "What? Why? Mr. Fortune seemed so nice at the party."

Gloria shook her head. "He is, but it's not Patrick Fortune I'll be working with," she said. "I'm talking about Jack Fortune."

"His son?" Confusion marred her perfect looks. "What's his son got to do with it?"

"Apparently everything." Gloria sighed as she broke a bread stick, more interested in the physical exercise than in eating it right now. "Mr. Fortune handed me over to him and I get the feeling that 'Sonny boy' is not too happy about the turn of events."

"I didn't know that Mr. Fortune had any mentally challenged children," Christina responded, clearly disturbed that someone didn't like Gloria.

Gloria laughed. Before their falling out, Christina had always been able to buoy her spirits with just a few choice words. God, she'd missed her, she thought now, lamenting the years that had been lost. "He doesn't. But he's certainly got at least one offspring who's definitely manners-challenged. Jack Fortune thinks he walks on water." She broke another bread stick into several pieces until it was almost reduced to crumbs. She kept envisioning the younger Fortune's neck with each snap. "And I'm not sure if I can hold my tongue until everything's ready to go."

As Gloria picked up a third bread stick, Christina tactfully took it out of her hands and bit off a piece.

"Well, you'd better. Mama said that Mr. Fortune was going to lend you any seed money you might need to get started. At three-percent interest," she emphasized. "You can't get a deal better than that."

Gloria concentrated to keep her mouth from falling open. Patrick had said nothing about a loan. She wondered if Jack knew and if that was why he was so cold toward her. "Three percent? Are you sure?"

Christina made short work of the bread stick and picked up another before Gloria could kill it. "I'm sure. Mama was very happy about it."

A former CPA with a company that had gone under, Gloria had done her homework and knew she had enough to cover everything for the move with some money to spare—as long as there were no unusual surprises. To discover that she now had a safety net was a tremendous relief. Armed this way, she knew she was capable of cutting the man's son a little slack. After all, it wasn't his fault he'd been born with a permanent scowl tattooed on his brow.

Gloria took a sip of water. "Patrick Fortune is a hell of a nice guy."

"Don't make 'em nicer," Christina agreed.

Gloria set her glass down, matching the bottom to the slight ring that had formed beneath it. "Too bad he couldn't have passed his 'nice' gene on to his son." And then she smiled as she looked at her sister. There was mischief in her look the way there had been when they were young, when they'd whispered their innermost secrets to one another in the dead of night while shrouded by sheets and darkness. "But I guess for three-percent interest I can dance with the devil for a while."

"Just as long as it's not slow dancing," Christina said, obviously thinking of their pact.

"No danger of that."

The waiter arrived with a bottle of wine. "This is the house special." Holding it as if he was cradling a baby in his hands, he presented it to both of them.

Gloria read the label. A small nibble of temptation waltzed through her, but she ignored it. Raising her eyes to the waiter, she shook her head. "None for me, thank you."

"None for me, either," Christina was quick to chime in.

Gloria knew Christina didn't want to seem insensitive.

"She'll have a glass," she told the waiter.

"Glory—" Christina protested as the waiter began to pour.

"Don't turn it down on my account, Tina. I'm not that weak," she assured her. "Besides, if being with Jack Fortune didn't drive me to drink, I guarantee you watching you have a glass or two isn't going to do it. I'm on safe ground."

But Christina was taking no chances. She waved the waiter away. "Two ginger ales, please," she instructed. Once he was gone, taking the half-filled glass of wine and bottle with him, Christina leaned in toward her sister. "I'm not too sure how safe that ground you're standing on is."

Gloria didn't follow her. "Come again?"

Christina nodded toward something behind her. "Incoming. Twelve o'clock high," she added.

Gloria turned in her chair.

Patrick Fortune was walking into the restaurant—with his son.

She closed her eyes, seeking strength. There seemed to be no getting away from the man today. Resigned, she shifted back in her chair. "Of all the restaurants in all the world, he had to walk into mine," she murmured under her breath.

Christina grinned. "You don't look a thing like Humphrey Bogart." And then, because she sensed that something was going on here that she didn't quite understand but that was obviously troubling her sister, she added, "This is what we get for coming into a restaurant that's located in the Fortune-Rockwell building." Wanting to spare her sister, she pointed out the obvious. "We haven't ordered yet, Glory." She leaned down to pick up her purse. "We could go somewhere else."

"And have you late getting back from lunch? I don't think so. You haven't been working here long enough to risk that. No, put your purse back down, Tina, we're staying here. I'll deal with my threatening bout of indigestion like a trooper."

Christina watched as the two men were shown to a table and then seated.

"You know, for a walking case of indigestion looking to happen, Jack Fortune is one hell of a good-looking specimen," Christina pointed out.

Gloria opened her menu and pretended to be interested in the various offerings that met the eye. "According to the Bible, so was Lucifer."

Christina laughed. "Same old Gloria, scissortongued to the end."

Gloria pretended to sniff at the description. "I'll have you know that I was the picture of sweetness and light at our meeting—even when he was treating me like an airhead."

About to open her own menu, Christina stared at her incredulously. "Did he talk to you?"

"At me," Gloria corrected. "He talked 'at' me. Like I said, the man thinks he walks on water and I am the pond scum beneath his feet."

Christina shook her head, clearly amused at the choice of words. "As I remember, you were also given to exaggeration."

"Not this time," Gloria said defensively. "Mr. Jack Fortune doesn't think I'm a worthy recipient of his expertise. I can see it in his eyes. I'm not really sure why he's doing it."

"Maybe because his father asked him to and he can't find a way to say no," Christina suggested.

"Maybe."

The waiter had returned with their ginger ales. Setting them down, he took their orders, punching appropriate buttons on something that resembled a Palm Pilot.

Her stomach in knots, Gloria ordered the chef's salad. She was afraid that she wouldn't be able to keep anything more substantial down.

"Well," she theorized once the waiter had left again, "the only really good thing about Jack's attitude is that at least I know I won't be in jeopardy."

"Jeopardy?" Christina echoed.

"Of breaking our pact. Working closely with a gorgeous male might have strained my resolve. But since the gorgeous male is also a holier-than-thou type, I figure I'm safe."

She glanced toward him—and discovered that he was looking straight at her. As her stomach tightened a notch, she was glad all she was having was the salad.

What was going on here? The man was clear across the room, but it was as if space and the people who inhabited it had somehow magically melted away.

As if there was no one else in the dining area but the two of them. Not her sister, not his father. No one. Just them.

How had she thought that his eyes were lifeless? They seemed to look right into her.

Electricity shimmied up and down her spine, sending out shock waves to mark its path.

She knew she would have shivered if the rest of her body hadn't felt as if it had suddenly been frozen in place. What had happened? A moment ago she'd felt so confident that this was the one handsome man she was completely immune to.

Pride goeth before a fall.

Chapter Five

"Earth to Gloria."

Gloria blinked as her sister's voice penetrated the fog that had descended over her brain. She realized that Christina was waving a hand in front of her eyes, obviously waiting for a reaction.

She cleared her throat, if not her head. "I'm sorry, were you saying something?"

Christina shook her head. "I could have quoted the entire Gettysburg Address and I don't think you would have heard a single word just now. Where were you?" She glanced in the direction that Christina had been staring but didn't see anything out of the ordinary. Just the Fortunes at their table. "You look flushed, Glory. Are you coming down with something?"

"God, I hope not," Gloria responded with feeling. Reaching for her ginger ale, she drank the contents until her glass was empty.

Christina took a second look over her shoulder, this time seeing that her sister's line of vision directly took in Jack Fortune. But she doubted if Gloria's sudden trancelike state had anything to do with the man, not after the way she'd just talked about him.

Still…

Maybe she should be scouting out maid's outfits for Gloria, Christina mused, suppressing a grin. It would be nice to have her apartment given a thorough cleaning and if there was one thing she'd learned, whatever Gloria did, she did thoroughly.

"You sure you're all right?" she pressed.

Gloria nodded a tad too vigorously. "I'm just preoccupied about the move back home."

That, she could accept. "You're entitled. I was a little up in the air when I moved back, too." The waiter returned with their orders and she paused until he retreated again. "It's not exactly a tiny step, rerouting your entire life."

Gloria's lips curved slightly. No, it wasn't, but she wasn't exactly a novice at it, either. "I should be used to that by now. I've done it—what? Four times if you count that disaster of a marriage I had."

"Let's not." Christina was more than happy to pretend it had never happened. From what she'd heard, Gary wasn't worthy of Gloria. "Did you check out that sublet I told you about?"

Shifting so that she couldn't see Jack without an effort, she focused her attention on her sister. And on her new apartment.

"Yes, and I can't thank you enough for that tip. We came to an agreement almost immediately. The place is mine as of yesterday." She'd already spent her first night there and, unlike other first nights in new places she'd lived in, she'd had no trouble sleeping.

Christina looked delighted at the news. "It'll feel more like home once your furniture gets here."

Gloria laughed shortly. "Not all that much furniture to make the trip." She'd packed up what few things she could still lay claim to and given a storage unit in Red Rock as a receiving address. She'd spent part of yesterday getting in touch with the moving company that had then had to get in touch with the movers who were en route to Texas to tell them to change their final destination.

Christina tried to make light of it. "You always did insist on not having much baggage."

"At least physically," Gloria specified. Mentally was another story, but she was working on it. She was working on it, she repeated silently as if thinking it twice would somehow reinforce the effort and the final result.

"Well, I don't know about you, but I certainly have room for dessert."

"I second that motion." Gloria deliberately forced a happy note into her voice, vainly trying to block out the fact that Jack Fortune was still looking at her and for some reason, that was creating goose bumps along her flesh. She could almost feel his eyes skimming along her body.

Up to this point, she'd thought her imagination was exclusively reserved for the jewelry she designed. She didn't particularly like this turn of events.

Padding around in bare feet, her soles meeting the highly polished wooden floor, Gloria patrolled the large loft as she got ready the next morning. Jack would be by in a few minutes to pick her up to take her to where her jewelry store was going to be. She couldn't help wondering if the contrary man would take exception to the location. Well, he could take exception all he wanted, she'd already signed the one-year lease.

Nerves had taken an eggbeater to her stomach. She wasn't sure if it had to do with the fact that she was fully immersed in her venture or that she was attracted to Jack Fortune.

"I'm not attracted to him, I'm not," she protested to the window in absence of anything live to talk to. "It's just a matter of deprivation, that's all."

It wasn't just alcohol that hadn't touched her lips in two years. She hadn't been with a man for that length of time, either.

She glanced at her reflection in the shell-framed mirror that hung just shy of the front door. She was wearing her hair down today. Was that a mistake? Did it detract from her professionalism?

"You avoid things that are bad for you, right?" she asked her reflection. The woman in the mirror nodded in agreement.

She'd decided long before making that pact with her sisters that men were definitely bad for her. At least, the kind of men she seemed doomed to keep selecting. Handsome men with gorgeous eyes and no substance, and ultimately, no heart.

When she'd first met Gary, she'd thought that he was going to be different. He'd given off such a solid, protective air those first few weeks. Granted she'd never been head over heels in love with him, but then, she'd told herself that kind of feeling belonged to the very young and the very delusional. She'd figured that Gary would be good for her and that for the rest of her life she'd be content if not wildly happy.

She'd been neither.

It wasn't long before she'd discovered that Gary's solid exterior and protective veneer were only that, a veneer. Beneath it the man she'd thought would be loving had turned out to be controlling instead. And, since she'd been easier to handle while under the influence, her wolf in prince's clothing had done everything he could to encourage all her self-destructive habits.

She combed her fingers through her hair, adding a little height. The reflection in the mirror was frowning at her. Her marriage and subsequent divorce made ump-teen strikes against her. That was when she'd decided that if her judgment was so bad, she just wasn't going to exercise it any longer. At least not where men were concerned. So she'd put a cork in the wine bottle and a lid on her feelings.

So far, it had proved to be a good decision. Once sober, she got a great deal more accomplished. And with her mind uncluttered by the baggage that being in-volved with someone created, she'd managed to turn an interest and a skill into a satisfying, successful career.

So here she was, back on what was practically her home turf, facing another challenge. She thought of Jack. As much as she hated to admit it, her longing for a rela-tionship far outweighed her desire for a drink two to one.

She supposed that was only human, longing for something you couldn't have.

"Focus on how much of an ass he is, Glory," she or-dered herself. Hunting for her shoes, she found them by the kitchen bar. She put one on. "Besides, he's cold as ice. The woman who tries to make it with him had bet-ter be wearing thermal underwear."

The idea made her laugh.

Just then the doorbell rang. Startled, she grabbed hold of the counter to keep from falling over as she tried to put on the other shoe.

"Coming," she called, half walking, half hopping to the door.

It took several steps to get the four-inch black mules

to fit snugly on her feet. Stopping to adjust her shirt, which had hiked up during her little impromptu dance-of-the-shoes, Gloria took a deep breath and braced herself as she placed her hand on the doorknob.

"Right on time," she announced brightly as she opened the door.

Jack sailed across the threshold, an emperor taking possession of all he surveyed. "I usually am." *Was that a snide remark about his being five minutes late for their first meeting?*

Warm as ever, she thought. "Nice to know," she commented. "Let me get my purse." She hurried back to the bar in the kitchen. For the time being, it was the only flat surface available.

Jack took a good long look around the apartment. It was actually a large loft with what appeared to be a couple of cubbyholes off to the side. He imagined that one of them was probably her bedroom. He was standing in what was the combined living room, kitchen, dining room area. The only piece of furniture in the space was a stool against the bar in the kitchen. Otherwise, there wasn't even a spot to sit.

Was her bedroom as barren?

The thought came out of nowhere and he banished it back to the same place. "Furniture not arrive yet?"

"What?" And then his words played back in her head and she realized what he was referring to. "No, it hasn't." Wearing a winter-white pullover sweater and skirt that, together, gave the impression of forming a dress, she shrugged carelessly. "Not that there's that much to arrive."

"Minimalist?"

"Something like that."

She saw him scrutinizing her face. The man should have been an interrogator for the CIA. "I thought you said your business was doing well."

She resisted the urge to tell him that none of this was his business. Ordinarily, that wasn't her style. She liked talking, liked learning about other people and didn't mind them learning about her. But there was something about this man that just seemed to bring out her worst side. She forced herself to be more than civil. She didn't want Jack to have anything to use against her when he reported back to his father as she assumed he was going to do.

"It is," she retorted proudly. A defensive note entered her voice. "It was my marriage that didn't go well."

He looked at her hand. There wasn't even a hint of a tan line where her ring would have once been. Which meant that her divorce was not a recent thing.

She saw where he was looking and wondered what was going through his head. Gloria made a calculated guess and decided to set the record straight. "I bought him off with furniture. He was more attached to it than I was, anyway. I do miss the TV, though."

"You don't have a TV?" He didn't watch much himself, other than CNN on occasion and then only to stay abreast of what was going on in the world, but he thought that all women were hooked on talk shows and daytime drama, taping it if they couldn't be there to watch the episode being aired.

"I do." Right now, it was on a crate in the bedroom. Right at the foot of the bedroll she'd borrowed from her brother. "But not like the one I gave up. Cost more than the first car I ever owned. Plasma," she told him since Jack had temporarily ceased to ask questions. Watching anything on the set was like actually being there. Even commercials were fun.

Gloria paused by the small closet just at the front door and took out her coat. Holding her sleeve with the same hand, she began to slip her arm into a coat sleeve. She felt Jack come up behind her and hold her coat so that she could get her other arm in more easily.

The close proximity brought another by-now-familiar wave of warmth up along her spine. She pulled back, stepping to the side and nearly bumping into the wall. Her heart skipped a beat. She raised her eyes to his, feeling amazingly clumsy.

"Thanks."

"Don't mention it." He followed her out the door, waiting as she locked up. Her three-quarter-length coat called his attention to her legs.

As if she needed help in having someone notice them, Jack thought, annoyed that his eyes had lingered there longer than should have been warranted.

"Let's get going," he snapped, taking the stairs down. There was, he'd discovered, no elevator to the fourth-floor apartment.

Gloria followed him down. "I thought that was what we were doing."

He said nothing. Reaching the first floor, he held the door for her only long enough for her to reach it, then strode outside. Jack led the way to his car.

Stopping by the passenger side, he opened the door and held it. This time he didn't abandon his post; he waited until she got in before closing the door and rounding the hood.

"Why are you doing this?" Gloria asked him as he got in behind the steering wheel.

Putting the key into the ignition, he turned it. The Jaguar purred to life. Right now, it was giving him a lot less grief than she was. "Because it's too far and too cold to walk to the address you gave me."

She'd given him the location of the store, which was in the midst of renovations, when he'd called early this morning to confirm their meeting. She'd had the same impression then as when she'd first met him.

As she had now.

"No, I'm not talking about driving to the jewelry store, I'm talking about becoming my business adviser in the first place."

Like a man comfortable with who and what he was, he answered simply and with no apology. "Because my father asked me to."

That wasn't good enough as far as she was concerned. She was accustomed to doing things alone and while she welcomed the Fortune stamp of approval and any leverage that association gave her in this highly competitive business, it wasn't going to be at the sake of her pride. She didn't need this man talking down to her, looking at her critically.

It was her shaky self-esteem that had been the culprit for her sliding down the slippery slope that had ultimately led to rehab in the first place.

"Look, it's very evident that you'd rather be running barefoot over hot coals, on your way to get a root canal, than helping me, so why don't we just call it a day? You can tell your father everything's all right and I'll just go about my business the way I did when I first got started in Denver."

Most people vied for the Fortune's backing. What was her angle? "Just like that?"

She faced forward and stared straight ahead, aware that he was looking at her. "Pretty much."

It made no sense. "I thought you asked for my father's help."

She wanted the record set straight. "No, my mother asked for your father's help." She knew that her mother had had only good intentions. She also knew it was futile to tell her mother to back off and stop worrying. Worrying, Maria Mendoza had told her time and again, was part of a mother's job description. "I guess she still worries about me. According to my mother, I am going to be her 'little girl' even when I blow out eighty-nine candles on my birthday cake."

He laughed dryly, doing his damnedest not to pay attention to the way her mouth curved fondly as she spoke of her mother. "I know how that is. Although my father does pretty much stay out of my business."

Was he talking about private or professional? "I thought it was his business—"

"It is, but lately I've been running the New York office according to my guidelines. In a way, that makes it mine." He stopped himself, realizing that he'd just admitted something to a woman he knew next to nothing about. A veritable stranger. That wasn't a habit with him.

"And you're dying to get back." It wasn't a guess, she could tell by the look in his eyes despite the restraint he was attempting to exercise. The New York office was his baby.

"'Dying' might be a tad dramatic," he informed her. "But I don't mind saying that I'm a city kid, born and bred."

He said that as if San Antonio wasn't worth his time. Texas pride prompted her next words. "San Antonio isn't exactly the sticks."

Maybe not, he allowed, but it certainly wasn't like New York City. "No, but New York has this energy, this verve—"

She found herself resenting his attitude. "Probably because everyone's so tense, waiting for someone to make a move on them."

Chauvinism made him take her words as a personal affront. If there was anything he hated, it was the way people insisted on running down New Yorkers. "You're stereotyping—"

"Aren't you?" she countered. "You make us sound like hicks."

"'Us'?" Hadn't she told him that she'd just moved here from Denver?

"I was born and raised in Red Rock."

He knew that. He also knew something else. "But you left."

The reasons for that were complex and plentiful. She wasn't about to go into it with a pompous know-it-all no matter who his father was.

"That's a story for another day. Besides—" her tone underscored the word "—I'm back." They were coming up to a busy intersection. She knew a shortcut that would circumvent what looked like a jam in the making. "Take a left here." And then she changed her mind. Not about the direction they were going, but about the direction of the day. "No, wait."

"Wait?" he echoed in disbelief. Did she think he could stop moving in the middle of all this? If he did, in two seconds they'd be surrounded with a cacophony of horns, all blasting at them.

"You can let me out on the corner." She pointed toward it. "I can walk the rest of the way."

He made no attempt to pull over. "Are you kicking me off this assignment?"

"No, I'm opening the door and letting you run away from this assignment, no disrespect intended," she added when he raised one dark eyebrow at the word "run."

Much as the idea tempted him, he had no intentions of backing out. He'd given his father his word and he was going to see this through. The woman was exhibiting about as much sense as an opossum in the middle of a busy five-lane road.

"Since we're almost there, I might as well take a look at the location you've picked."

Nope, she definitely didn't like his attitude. The sooner she was rid of this man, the better she was going to feel. On several levels.

"You make it sound like I'm a kid with a whim. I did a lot of scouting around before I decided on this mall. I also took overhead into account," she added. "The ideal location for my shop is at the San Antonio Mall, but the leases there are a little pricey. I thought I'd get a foothold here first, then work my way over in about a year or three."

She had actually thought it out, he realized. "I'm impressed."

Did he really think that mattered to her? "Oh, good. I can die happy."

The sarcasm was thick enough to cut with a knife. And his patience was wearing thin. "Anyone ever tell you that you have a smart mouth?"

Was that his best comeback? The man might as well hang up his gloves now, she'd won the match. "Not lately. It goes with the rest of me."

Making a right at the corner, Jack snorted. "Well, your ego's alive and well."

"No thanks to you." The words had come out before she could stop herself.

He looked at her, surprised. "What do I have to do with it?"

"You've done nothing but talk down to me since the elevator encounter."

"I asked you to press the thirtieth floor." How could she possibly see that as talking down to her? Was she paranoid?

"No," she pointed out, her voice steely, "you snapped out the number."

"Oh, for pity's sake—" He got hold of his temper. Even so, he snapped the next words out. "I was fighting jet lag."

It had obviously not been much of a fight from what she'd seen. "Sounds like the jet lag won." Turning her face forward again, her eyes widened as she saw a maroon Chevy coming from the right, running the light. She braced her feet hard against the floor. "Watch out!"

But it was already too late.

A half second after the warning was out of her mouth, the front of Jack's silver Jaguar made contact with the side of the car that had flown out of nowhere. The Chevy, at least fifteen years old, dented and its paint peeling in half a dozen places, was the heavier of the two vehicles. The impact sent the silver Jaguar spinning in a full circle, winding up exactly at the original point of contact.

The next moment, a sound like rushing water filled the interior of the car. Jack's vision was completely blocked by a wall of white fabric.

The air bags had deployed.

Along with what remained of his already frayed patience.

Chapter Six

There was white everywhere.

Panic clawed sharply at Gloria's throat. She felt as if she had been plunged into the center of a marshmallow.

Claustrophobia, a failing she hadn't managed to conquer that accompanied her into every elevator, every small space she found herself in since she'd been six years old, rose up on its hoary hind legs to grab her by the throat and threaten to block out the very air into her lungs.

The fact that the air bag had her pressed back against her seat with no room for movement and the seat belt was biting into her shoulder and lap, holding her fast, only added to the tidal wave of panic that was building up inside her.

She couldn't help her next reaction. It came without thinking, without warning. Gloria started to scream. Not a small gasp or a yelp, but a full-bodied, blood-curdling scream that could have shattered water glasses within a one-mile radius.

Jolted, Jack's senses alert and at their peak, the scream ripped right through him. Heart pounding, he could only imagine what could have prompted that sort of a reaction from the woman who was completely blocked from his sight. Memories of the car accident with Ann came bursting back into his brain.

Ann screaming.

Just before she died.

Terror seized his heart. Struggling, pushing against the deployed air bag, Jack managed to unbuckle his seat belt and get the harness off his shoulder. Adrenaline running high, convinced that Gloria had to be severely hurt, possibly even dying, he groped for the door handle on his side. Locating it seemed to take forever. Finally successful, Jack yanked on it and applied his shoulder to the door, shoving his way out.

"Hang on!" he yelled to Gloria as he rounded the trunk.

Operating on two very distinct planes, he saw the offending driver and glared at him. Jack could just barely make out the man's face. The other car engine was still running and the driver looked ready to make a break for it. Now.

"Don't even think it!" Jack barked. Making his way to the passenger side of the Jaguar, he glanced quickly at the other car's license plate, committing it to memory. A photographic memory allowed him to absorb and retain everything he had ever seen. "I've got your plate number and I swear I'll hunt you down."

The man behind the wheel of the dented Chevy froze and raised his hands in surrender. He began to babble an apology. His words were just so much noise in the background. Jack barely heard him.

All of his attention was focused on Gloria.

If she could scream like that, at least she was alive, he thought, taking comfort in that. The very hair on the back of his neck was standing on end as the sound skewered its way through his system.

Jack yanked open her door. He groped around the air bag, trying to find Gloria's hand. "It's okay, I've got you. It's okay," he told her over and over again.

The panic wouldn't leave even as she heard his voice. Her terror was too huge to overcome. In saner times, it bothered her no end, reacting this way, but right now, all she could do was shriek.

"Pull me out," she pleaded. "Pull me out!"

And then she felt a hand reaching across her waist, brushing against her lap. The next moment, the belt that was holding her prisoner was released and she was being pulled out of her living tomb.

The second she was clear of the car, she began gasping for air, sucking it in as if there wasn't even an ounce of it within her lungs. Her legs weak, her body a heavy liquid, she clung to the man who had pulled her free.

Shaking, she was still aware of the soft feel of suede against her cheek and the infinite comfort of the arms that had locked around her. She fought to regulate her breathing.

"Where are you hurt?" Jack demanded. Had she hit her head? Broken something in the split second before the air bag had cocooned her?

When Gloria didn't answer, Jack tried to move her back and hold her at arm's length to see her injuries for himself. At first she wouldn't let go of him, her arms locked around his neck in a death grip. Finally he managed to gently but firmly push her from him.

"Where are you hurt?" he asked again. Scanning her face, he saw nothing. There were no scratches, no cuts, no marks at all except for what appeared to be the beginning of a slight bruise along her forehead. That could have come from the air bag itself, he judged. But one thing was abundantly clear. The dark-haired woman he'd been verbally sparring with not a few minutes earlier was clearly shaken.

That made two of them, he thought.

And then, suddenly, there were people crowding all around them in the intersection.

"I saw the whole thing," one man behind him volunteered.

A woman in a flaming-red scarf that was wrapped around her neck pointed to the other driver. "It was his fault." The accusation was made in a high-pitched voice.

A businessman craned his neck as he leaned out of

his car window. His vehicle was directly behind the bruised Jaguar. "Need a witness?"

Voices were coming from all sides, swelling in volume. Gloria tried to block them all out as she struggled to regain her composure. She was only vaguely aware of Jack leading her to the sidewalk. She followed him like some docile child, hating this role she'd been forced to play. Hating the way she'd reacted. Still unable to do anything else.

She'd completely lost it back there and she was ashamed of that. But it had felt as if she was being buried alive.

Jack was taking her face in his hands, examining it closely. Was he trying to figure out what kind of a lunatic his father was lending money and support to?

Gloria felt like an idiot but her heart refused to stop racing.

"You okay?" he asked gruffly.

The gruff voice helped to center her, pulling her out of crisis mode. But still, she didn't trust her voice to answer so she merely nodded in response.

"Okay, stay right here," he instructed her before glancing over his shoulder at the other driver, "while I get some insurance information out of Mario Andretti over there."

A ring of Good Samaritans and people looking for some excitement had surrounded the offending driver. No one seemed inclined to allow the man to leave. Jack quickly got the necessary information from the driver, who kept babbling his apology, claiming the sun had gotten into his eyes and could they please keep this off the record so his insurance wouldn't go through the roof?

From the way the other man was talking, Jack got the impression that this wasn't the man's first offense.

It made his blood boil. Someone so careless should be kept off the road.

Maybe if you'd kept Ann off the road, she'd still be here today.

Jack blocked out the thought even as it echoed in his brain. He couldn't go there yet. He suspected that he probably never fully could.

Jack looked at the other man coldly, feeling not even an ounce of pity. He hated recklessness and the man had clearly run the light. "My insurance agent will be in touch."

Flipping open his phone, he called for roadside assistance. He wasn't about to go anywhere with the air bags deployed, even if they were now in the process of deflating. Besides, who knew the kind of damage his car had sustained? There was no way he was about to take the road with an unsafe vehicle.

Pocketing the cell phone, he took a few names from the bystanders in case the insurance adjuster would require the testimony of witnesses. He'd learned a long time ago to cover as many bases as was humanly possible. The other driver was sitting moodily in his vehicle, muttering something about hard-nosed businessmen who thought they owned the road. Jack could feel his temper flaring, but he ignored him. There was nothing to be gained by stooping to the driver's level.

What counted was that no one was hurt.

Gloria had given him one hell of a scare, he thought, looking over at her. Finished taking information, he tucked his Palm Pilot into his pocket and crossed back to the woman standing on the curb.

She looked calmer now. That wild look he'd seen in her eyes was gone. Still, he wasn't completely at ease about her. The sound of a siren began to cut through the din. Someone had either called the paramedics or the police. Probably both.

"You want to go to the hospital?" he asked Gloria. Funny, he hadn't thought of her as fragile until now. Like fine china about to crack.

She shook her head, trying to regain her self-esteem. It was at times like this, when everything felt so out of control, that she reverted back to who and what she'd been just two years ago. A woman too weak-willed to make it from one end of the day to the other without help.

You're a whole new person since then. Remember that.

She shook her head as she squared her shoulders. "No, I'm all right."

He appeared not to believe her as his eyes seemed to bore holes right through her. "Are you sure? You were screaming back there as if you were being filleted."

That was a pretty apt description of it, she thought.

Not that she had any control over her reaction. Lord knew, she wished she had.

Gloria took a deep breath and looked away, avoiding his probing eyes. She supposed she owed him some kind of an explanation. She kept it at a minimum. Her voice was hardly above a whisper as she said, "I have claustrophobia."

Jack cocked his head as if he hadn't heard her. "What?"

Frustrated, Gloria pressed her lips together. She'd managed to put everything else in her life in order, but this was a failing, a shortcoming from her childhood, and she hated it because there was no way she had ever managed to exercise any control over it. For the most part, she tried to think of other things when she couldn't avoid a situation such as riding up in elevators to floors that were too high up to walk to.

But with this accident there had been no time to prepare. It had stripped her of all her little mind-diverting tricks and left her naked and vulnerable.

"I have claustrophobia," she repeated more clearly. Her teeth were clenched as she strained the admission through them.

He passed his hands lightly along her arms and shoulders, as if her word was not enough. "So nothing's damaged or broken," he pressed.

"Nothing's damaged or broken," Gloria confirmed. And then she added in a less audible voice, "Except maybe my self-esteem."

He surprised her by shrugging away her admission.

If she didn't know any better, she would have said he was being kind.

"Hey, everyone's got something." The crowd around them was dispersing. The siren grew louder. This was going to take a while. "If you won't go to the hospital, want me to call a cab to take you home?"

She was getting her wind back. And with it, her determination. "No, I still have to show you the store location."

He looked at her, surprised that she could think of that after what had just happened. She could have been killed. She needed time to process that. And he needed time to put it out of his mind. "We can postpone the trip."

She squared her shoulders again, reminding him of a soldier on the battlefield determined to face his fears. And his enemy. He wondered if he fell under that category and why that seemed to bother him.

"I don't want to," she informed him crisply.

There were several strands of hair hanging in her face. Jack had no idea what possessed him to gently brush them back. Or why the simple gesture brought a wave of heat surging through him, beginning with his loins and radiating out. The day was inordinately cold.

Maybe he was suffering from shock and didn't realize it. The scenario that had just transpired was chillingly similar to the one that had taken place nearly twenty years ago.

Except that then it had been Ann who was driving.

Ann who had insisted on taking a joyride while still feeling the effects of an afternoon's worth of partying. He'd gone with her when he hadn't been able to get her to surrender her car keys. Maybe it had been the brashness of youth, the brashness that convinced every one of them that they were immortal, that nothing could happen to them because they were young and full of promise. Whatever it was, he felt she'd be safe if he went with her.

A lot he knew.

Running a light, just as this man had, she'd hit a driver. He remembered the horror that had spiked through him, the awful noise of metal crashing against metal. And most of all, he remembered Ann's scream. The last sound she'd ever made. She and the driver were both dead at the scene. And him? He'd gotten a cluster of minor injuries that had landed him in the hospital for a couple of weeks.

Physically, the injuries had been minor. Emotionally was another story. He'd wanted to die, to be with Ann for all eternity. But all he'd sustained were things that could heal.

Other than his heart.

He had absolutely no patience with people who drank to the point that the alcohol controlled them instead of the other way around. And although there'd been no alcohol on the breath of the other driver, the man had still been reckless and run the light.

Gloria was looking at him almost defiantly. He made

up his mind. "All right. Once the guy from roadside assistance gets here and we're finished giving our statements to the police, I'll call a cab and we can go see about the location. If you're sure you're all right," he added again.

Exasperation filled her voice as a policeman got out of his patrol vehicle. "You don't have to keep asking that. I'm not going to change my story."

Stubborn. He supposed that was a good sign. Jack cupped his ear as he tilted his head toward hers. "'Fraid you're going to have to speak up. You blew out my ears in the car."

Gloria looked at him sharply. She could make out a hint of a smile on his lips.

He was making a joke.

That stunned her almost as much as his gentleness had. "I didn't know you had a sense of humor."

He leaned in even closer to her, his hand still cupped around his ear. "What?"

She laughed, the tension finally beginning to leave her. Just in time to give her statement to the policeman approaching them.

Forty minutes later, after renting a car, they were finally standing inside a shop on the second floor of the Big T Mall. Until a month ago, the space had been occupied by a trendy baby clothing store. Doing well, the owner had decided to move on to a better location. The pink and blue lettering on the glass door had been scraped off just that morning. There was scaffolding on either side of the entrance and the modest interior was in a complete state of chaos.

In the three days since she had begun leasing the space, thanks to Patrick Fortune backing her bank loan, she'd had to forward ten different bewildered customers on to the store's new location. Each had said something about thinking the store would remain at that location forever. One woman had obviously made good use of the place. She'd had four children with her. Two in stroller, two hanging off the stroller. And if that bulge Gloria had noted was any indication, a fifth on the way.

She hoped that someday her customers would come looking for her store like that, loyally searching for her only to be told of a more high-end address.

She wondered if any of her clients in Denver would make the trip out, or try to get in touch with her via the store's Web site.

Right now, what seemed to matter most—and she really didn't understand why it meant anything to her one way or another—was the stamp of approval from the man roaming the unfinished store.

She held her breath as she watched Jack look around. All signs of the previous store were gone, except for one two-dimensional cardboard rendition of a crawling baby the owner had decided to leave behind. It was leaning off to the side. She thought of it as her good-luck charm, a leftover from a successful business.

Nerves danced through her, a parent watching her child being judged, as she watched Jack survey the area. So far, there was no indication of what the store was planning to evolve into. But it was still early days.

Finally, his feet firmly planted on a drop cloth, he glanced at her over his shoulder. "This the best location you could find?"

All traces of the man who had rescued her from her marshmallow grave seemed to have vanished in smoke. They were back in their individual sparring corners, she thought.

Maybe it was better this way. For a few minutes back there, she'd actually liked him. Coupling that with the physical attraction that seemed to insist on existing, refusing to disappear, made for a dangerous combination. This overly critical version of Jack Fortune, JF Version 1.0 she thought with a smile, was one she could more easily resist.

What she might have trouble resisting right now, she thought, was wrapping her hands around his throat and choking him every time he opened his condescending mouth. Each time he did, she winced inwardly, bracing herself for yet another derogatory comment. It was getting damn hard to smile at him.

"Is it the best location I could find?" she echoed his question, knowing it annoyed him. "In my price range, yes, it is." And then she felt compelled to defend her decision. "Besides, the last business that was here did very well."

He looked around slowly and she had no way of guessing what he was thinking. Only something bad. "Another jewelry store?" he finally asked.

She pointed to the cardboard figure leaning against the back wall. "A baby clothing store." And then she saw him frown. *Great, now what?*

He crossed back to her, his hands shoved deep into the pants' pockets of his custom-made suit. "You're comparing apples and oranges."

She shook her head. "No fruit involved," she answered tartly. "I was thinking of foot traffic." She wished she could remember the numbers. Annoyance had temporarily wiped the stats from her brain. "This mall sees a lot of people. Most of the stores here do well." And then, suddenly remembering the numbers, she rattled them off to him.

He looked at her for a long moment and she could feel her blood pressure rising.

"You've done your homework," he finally conceded.

There it was again, that sarcastic edge in his voice. Damn it, no matter how attractive and sexy this man looked, his attitude ruffled her feathers. Any vague temptation she might have been entertaining went up in smoke the second Jack Fortune opened his mouth.

"Thank you," she replied coldly to his homework comment. "But it is my dime."

"And my father's," he reminded her. "He is lending you any extra money you might need."

Her eyes narrowed. Was he going to bring that up at

every opportunity? Of course he was. "All the more reason to do my homework."

"Yes, it is."

Jack inclined his head, signaling an end to the round. He was sparring with her and he knew why. It all stemmed from the car accident. He'd felt the need to protect her. And he'd felt responsible for her. It went deeper than just being responsible for someone fate threw him together with. He felt something for *her.*

Undoubtedly the feelings he'd experienced had all been brought on by memories of Ann, but he still didn't like the wave of panic that had assaulted him when he'd first heard Gloria screaming. Moreover, he definitely didn't like the odd sensation that had waltzed through him, filling every cavity, when she'd clung to him after he'd extracted her from the vehicle.

Things had stirred inside him. Things with cobwebs and dust on them.

Feelings.

The last thing he wanted awakened within him were feelings. The sooner this woman was out of his hair, the better.

Chapter Seven

"So, how's it going?"

There was no need for any sort of a preamble. Jack knew exactly what the "it" was that his father was referring to. He was talking about Gloria and her jewelry store.

His father had called him at his Plaza Hotel suite earlier and asked him to swing by the office this morning. Though he wasn't an optimist by nature, a small part of Jack had hoped that there would be something in the offing beyond the assignment that had brought him to San Antonio in the first place.

One look at his father's expression had permanently sunk that hope.

Again he couldn't help but wonder why his father was so intense about the success or failure of this woman's business. Granted his father was a very charitable man—Jack doubted if anyone gave as much to charity as his parents did—but this somehow went beyond the call.

Jack shrugged, sinking his hands deep into his pockets as he wandered around the office, studying the paintings his father had chosen to keep him company while he was in San Antonio.

He'd heard somewhere that his father was considering having Derek take over this office when his father went back to New York. Even though he meant to return there himself—and as fast as possible—he couldn't help feeling just the slightest bit piqued that his father would even be considering Derek for the top position instead of him.

Although he and Derek were as close as two friends could be, there was more than a healthy sort of rivalry between them. It was what kept his brain honed, he told himself.

"All things considered," Jack replied, moving on to another painting, this one a more dramatic Turner seascape, "I'd rather be back in New York."

Patrick's fingers ceased flying over the keyboard as he looked up at his son and shook his head. "You move too fast, Jack. Stop a minute, catch your breath."

Jack looked at his father over his shoulder. He was irritable because he was standing still, not moving fast. "I'm not out of breath."

His words had absolutely no effect on his father. "Denial's a sure sign that you're even worse off than you thought you were."

Abandoning the next painting, Jack crossed to his father's desk and leaned over it, digging his knuckles in on the blotter. "Dad, I *like* work."

Patrick's expression softened, lessening the lines around his eyes. "I know you do, and I appreciate that. There's nothing more satisfying than earning a living at what you like and what you're good at."

"But?" The word literally seemed to be throbbing in the space between them.

Jack was a workaholic of the first water, but that just meant Patrick had to work harder to get through to him. Now that his own soul had been saved, thanks to his wife, he refused to abandon Jack. "But you can't take it home with you at night."

Jack laughed shortly. There, he had his father, he thought. "Sure you can. Between laptops, PDAs and the Internet—"

Patrick raised a warning brow. "You know what I mean. You need a family."

Jack threw up his hands. This was getting annoying. He thought only women had to listen to this kind of thing from their mothers. He would have bet anything that his father was above this kind of nonsense. Obviously he would have lost that bet.

"I *have* a family, Dad. I've got you and Mom and those annoying people you keep telling me are my siblings." He allowed himself a grin. He cared a great deal for his brothers and baby sister, he just wasn't about to try to duplicate them by creating children. "I'd say that's family enough for anyone."

Patrick's eyes locked with his son's. "A family of your own, Jack."

Jack gave his father an innocent look. "Were you and Mom on loan?"

"A wife, Jack. A wife," his father emphasized. Before Jack could say anything, Patrick added, "And kids. Lots of kids."

Restless, Jack moved to the window. The rain that had been threatening since yesterday had finally arrived. Sheets of water were lashing against the window. The world outside looked dreary. The world inside wasn't much better, he thought.

"I don't know if I'd be any good at that," he said, addressing his words to his father's reflection in the window.

"Well, you certainly won't find out by hiding behind corporate reports."

Jack whirled around. No one had ever even hinted that he was a coward. He felt a sharp flare of temper and managed to bank it down. "Not hiding, Dad, analyzing. It's what I do. What you pay me to do, remember?"

Patrick used the opportunity to swing the conversation back onto its original track. "Speaking of which, how's that venture with Gloria Mendoza going?"

He noticed that his father had conveniently dropped

the woman's married name. Had Gloria gone through legal channels to do that, or was his father just trying to set something in motion here, make him think of her as a single woman?

No, that couldn't be right. He and his father had an open, honest relationship. His mother might attempt a little manipulation with romance as the goal, but not his father. They were too alike, he and his father, even though the man seemed to have temporarily taken leave of his senses.

He told his father what was foremost in his mind. "I still think you should have handed this little assignment off to someone else." He didn't even have to think about who he'd get in place of himself. "Like Derek. He's got more patience than I do."

For a moment Patrick said nothing. Instead he thought of how he'd arranged to have his one-time protégé hire Gloria's sister to act as his business analyst. It would have been a lie to say that he didn't feel quite proud of himself. With a little bit of luck, things should be percolating there, as well.

His answer to Jack was vague. "Derek's got his hands full with other projects."

Did his father view him as a spoiled, pampered, rich offspring? Hadn't he proven himself over and over again to be invaluable? "And I don't?"

"I told you before, Jack, this needs your touch." *And, if I don't miss my guess, so does Gloria. Almost as much as you need hers.*

Jack scrutinized his father's face. He could almost see the words marching through his brain. See them, but not quite make them out.

Or maybe he didn't want to, because that would be giving credence to something he felt shouldn't be going on. "What are you thinking?"

Patrick leaned back in his chair, studying his firstborn. Jack had never given him one moment's trouble. Maybe there was such a thing as being too perfect, Patrick decided.

"That you're a chip off the old block. That at your age, I was determined not to slow down, either. But I discovered that I was competing against myself. You can't win if you have yourself as your opponent."

Jack laughed shortly. That was true enough. But so was something else. "You also can't lose."

Doing nothing but work extracted a toll on a person's life. And work, Patrick had come to realize, was a cold mistress. "Depends on your definition of losing."

"I don't have a definition of losing," Jack told his father glibly. "Because I never intend to lose."

Patrick looked at his son for a long moment. Anyone else would have said the man was too cocky, that he needed to be taken down a peg. But Patrick knew that Jack was as good as his word. And failure was not an option with Jack.

Maybe not, but a little humility was in order.

"I hope not, Jack," he said softly. "I sincerely hope not."

There *was* something going on, Jack thought, but he wasn't exactly sure just what. The old man was acting funny these days. It was more than just his laid-back attitude about the company. Granted, if there was a crisis, the way there had been many times in the past, his father would be right there in the thick of it, leading the charge, rallying his subordinates. Jack smiled to himself. No one did it better than the old man.

But when everything was going relatively smoothly, his father tended to, for lack of a better term, slack off. Maybe age was finally catching up with him. Jack couldn't help wondering if it was time for his father to step down.

The very thought saddened him. No matter what his father said, Fortune-Rockwell represented the sum total of his life's work. The senior Fortune would go out of his mind if he retired. No, better to have him where he was and, if necessary, he could pick up the slack for his father. After all, it wasn't as if there was anything more important to Patrick than the company.

Unexpectedly, a strange, hollow feeling made itself evident for just a split second.

Is that all there is? At the end of the day, is that all there is?

He'd been paying too much attention to his father, Jack thought. Not everyone was cut out for a wife and kids, no matter what his father thought. The one love of his life was dead, and he damn well had no intentions of looking for a substitute.

Glancing at his father, he saw that the latter looked as if he was gearing up again. Jack moved to leave. "I guess I'll go see how your project is doing."

Jack saw his father's mouth pull into a satisfied smile. He doubted if it had to do with the speech he was supposed to be writing. But he isn't about to ask.

"Good idea," was all he said to Jack's departing back.

The sooner he was done, Jack told himself as he parked on the far side of the mall, the sooner he could get out of Dodge, or San Antonio as it were, and back to the fast-paced life he thrived on in New York.

Maybe that was what his father needed, as well, he mused. To get out of here and get back into the mainstream, back to New York where business was business and everything else came in second.

He walked in through one of the four department stores that made up the quadrangle that defined the mall. His mind elsewhere, he made his way to the inner core of the mall without noticing any of the displays.

But as he hurried along the second floor of the mall, his surroundings sank in despite his preoccupation. He realized that Gloria had been right. There *were* a lot of people frequenting the mall. It was a weekday. The stores had only been open for about an hour and yet there were a great many people milling around, shopping, socializing, on their way to one place or another. Since it was neither lunchtime nor a holiday, he figured this had to represent an average day.

Blind luck?

No, that was a bit harsh, he thought. He had to give the woman her due. Talking to her, he'd come away with the feeling that although she seemed bullheaded, she also seemed to have something on the ball.

He'd done a little poking around into her background, looking into her past business dealings. From all appearances, she had done well in Denver. And there was every indication that she would have continued to do well had she remained there.

But she'd chosen to move back to Texas and start over again. Why?

Was it just to get away from an ex-husband and come home, or something else? Were there memories that haunted her, causing her to leave?

He could understand that. When Ann had died so suddenly, leaving him in an emotional abyss, he'd almost dropped out. He'd found himself unable to deal with seeing her face everywhere he went, remembering the times they'd spent together. It had been hell. If he hadn't had only one semester to go and his father hadn't been so persuasive, he might very well have just given in to his desire to become a beach bum.

Who was he kidding? He was far too much of a type A personality to be content sipping drinks out of a hollowed-out coconut shell and make that his life's preoccupation.

So why had Gloria decided to suddenly uproot everything and start all over again? That was something he hadn't been able to find out. He didn't believe she'd just wanted to come home again. You went where the money was.

Reaching her shop, he saw that the glass doors no longer afforded a view of the interior. There was paper taped to the inside to keep passersby from looking in. Given her personality, he found that somewhat unusual. She struck him as someone who enjoyed an audience.

Jack tried the door and it gave.

Leaving the door unlocked was more like her, he mused. The next moment the realization that he thought himself familiar enough with the woman to be able to second-guess her stopped him in his tracks. He had no idea what she was capable of, he silently insisted.

Slipping inside, he saw that rather than a team of people, there was only one worker around, a slender youth bending over a can of paint, preparing to pour the contents into a paint tray. He had on a cap, pulled down low, and there was periwinkle-blue paint drizzled all over his coveralls.

The other workers were probably on a break, taking advantage of the woman, he decided. Good thing he'd decided to show up. Apparently she only knew how to order around one person at a time.

Coming up behind the youth, he addressed the painter's back. "Excuse me, do you know where I can find Gloria Johansen?"

Startled, the painter swung around. The radio was turned on and although the music was soft, it had obviously masked any noise he might have made entering the store.

A grin flashed and he recognized it instantly. "What's it worth to you?"

He scowled. Up close, he noticed the figure, even in coveralls, was pretty curvy. "Gloria."

She set down the roller and laughed as she picked up a towel to dry her hands. "And here I thought you didn't recognize me."

He wished she'd stop smiling. It was infinitely more difficult hanging on to his annoyance with her smiling at him like that. "What are you doing?"

She pretended to consider the question. "Well, let's see. Coveralls, paint, roller—I'll take a wild stab at it and say I'm painting."

"I know you're painting." He bit the words off. "Why are you painting?"

"Because I'm good at it," she answered glibly, her eyes twinkling as she added in a hushed, amused tone, "And—and you'll like this part," she assured him, placing a hand on his wrist to keep him in place, a move that was far too familiar for his liking. "Because I can save money doing it myself."

His frown only deepened, as did his annoyance. And yet part of him admired her enthusiasm. Not that he'd ever admit that, of course. "Don't you have other things to do?"

"Lots," she said. "And this was supposed to be going faster, but my brother dropped out on me." She looked at him and obviously decided that he needed more information. "Jorge was supposed to come by to help but he was distracted at the last minute."

He swore that every third sentence out of her mouth was an enigma. He needed a codebook to understand what she was saying. "Distracted?"

Her tone was resigned, forgiving. "I'm afraid that my brother's libido is larger than his sense of responsibility when it come to promises he makes to his little sister." Gloria moved her shoulders in a careless shrug beneath the coarse coveralls. "Maybe it's for the best. He can be rather sloppy." And then her eyes lit up again and she looked at him as though suddenly seeing him for the first time. He felt as if he was watching the birth of an idea. "You, on the other hand, would probably do an excellent job."

He caught on before the sentence was out of her mouth. "If you're trying to go all Tom Sawyer on me, I'm afraid it's not going to work." There were a hundred things he would do before agreeing to pick up a paintbrush or a roller.

Undaunted, she pressed on. He had a feeling that other than tight spaces, very little daunted this woman.

"As I recall, Tom Sawyer pretended he was having so much fun that the other boys begged him to let them try their hand at it and even offered to trade things for the privilege of whitewashing his aunt Polly's fence." She opened her eyes wide, the very picture of innocence. A picture he wasn't buying. "I wouldn't presume to try to suck you into doing something with a lie."

She was a clever woman. Was she being transparent on purpose? "No, you'd use flattery."

The innocent expression remained intact. "No way. Just observation. You're a type A personality. You believe in being hands-on and you need to oversee everything yourself. People like that are too intense not to be good. Am I right?"

He watched in fascination as the smile on her lips blossomed and subsequently moved into her eyes. He supposed it wasn't only Irish eyes, as the old song went, that smiled, but dark, mesmerizing Mexican ones, as well.

He found he had to force words to his lips. "I've never painted anything in my life."

She nodded, as though expecting him to say as much. He felt as if he was involved in some kind of cosmic chess game.

"It's not hard, really. You just put paint on the roller." She picked one up to demonstrate, moving the roller up and down in the paint tray. "These rollers don't allow you to drip and they absorb just the right amount to cover a given space." She raised her eyes to his face. "You almost can't fail."

The look in her eyes dared him.

He found part of himself actually entertaining the idea and wondered if the paint fumes were getting to him. In the background he heard Blondie singing "'I'm gonna getcha, getcha, getcha...'"

"I'll get my suit dirty," Jack continued.

She spread her hands to her sides. "Not a problem. I've an extra set of coveralls." She nodded over to the side.

He didn't bother looking to verify. For the moment, she had captivated his attention. He told himself he could walk away anytime he chose. So, for the time being, he chose to remain.

"You come prepared."

"They were for Jorge." Her eyes slid slowly from his head to his toes. Her smile widened as a tinge of triumph highlighted it. "I'd say that you were about his height, give or take an inch."

"How convenient." Maybe this woman could have shown old Tom Sawyer a trick or two, he thought, amused despite himself.

Her smile warmed him as it washed over him. "Yes, isn't it? They're in the back room if you feel like trying them on."

He didn't move an inch. "And why would I want to do that?"

Her answer came without hesitation. The space between them, he noted, seemed to have been whittled down to nothing without either of them taking another step.

"So that you can conquer something else," she told him.

He wasn't altogether sure if she was talking about painting or if "something else" referred to a whole different subject entirely. All he knew was that the chemistry that seemed to act up every time he got within ten feet of her was present as always.

She stood waiting for his answer. Her expression indicated that she was rather certain of the outcome. He knew he should just turn on his heel and walk out. That would have been the smart thing to do. After all, he didn't like the smell of paint and he was far too busy a man to waste his time dipping a roller into a tray of periwinkle-blue liquid.

Finally, with a shrug, he turned away from her. But instead of heading for the papered doors, he walked in the opposite direction, toward the back.

So he'd try something new, he told himself.

He supposed Gloria was to be commended for trying to cut corners and save money. That made her a decent businesswoman. It was in keeping with what he'd already found out about her.

And he'd lied to her. He had painted before. He'd helped one of his roommates paint their dorm room while he was in college. They'd painted one wall stark black, the other three walls a virgin white. It had been very dramatic at the time. Now he had a feeling it would have driven him crazy.

He found the coveralls hanging on the inside of the back room door. Shedding his jacket and tie, he pulled the garment over his slacks and shirt.

"You're right." He snapped shut the row of snaps that ran along his chest. The coveralls felt a little tight, but not as bad as they could have. He could still move his arm. "Your brother and I are just about the same size…"

His voice trailed off as he came out of the back room and saw her balancing herself on the next-to-the-topmost rung on the ladder. Was she crazy? "What the hell are you doing up there?"

She turned around slowly to look down at him from the top of the ladder. Humor curved the corners of her mouth. "Am I going to have to explain this all over to you again? I'm painting."

"No, you're not," he corrected, really angry. "You're risking breaking your neck."

He wasn't just a type A personality, she thought, he was a worrier. She bristled against his implication that she was too clumsy to be careful.

"I'm standing on a ladder—A does not exactly equal B here."

He wasn't going to debate this with her. "Get down," he ordered.

Humor vanished. Her eyes narrowed into slits. He should have picked up on the warning, but he could almost see her flying off the ladder. "You're not in charge of me, Fortune."

He had a different opinion. "I am when you don't make an effort to use your brains and right now, they appear to be taking a break."

"For your information, I've climbed ladders before, Fortune." Open space had never been a problem for her. She had absolutely no fear of heights.

"Only means your luck is that much closer to running out." Crossing the floor, he came up to the ladder and stood right beneath her. "Now get down."

Anger surged through her. She stubbornly refused to budge. "Damn it, Jack, why do you insist on always seeing the glass as half empty?"

"Because it usually is. Now get down," he ordered again.

Gloria was sorely tempted to give him a piece of her mind, but she didn't want to alienate his father and most fathers didn't relish hearing that their sons compared to jackasses.

She blew out a breath. "All right, I'm coming down, but only because I need to refill my roller."

"Whatever." He held the ladder braced as she made her way down. In his opinion, she was moving awfully fast.

She was moving faster than that when she hit the next-to-the-last rung. Missing it, she slipped and went sailing off.

Right into his arms.

Chapter Eight

Sheer instinct had guided his movements. Jack caught her without thinking. One second he was standing below Gloria, the next she'd somehow twisted around and was airborne.

The ladder she'd involuntarily vacated wobbled dangerously for a second, but mercifully remained standing upright. Jack hardly noticed. He was too busy assessing the immediate situation. That he was holding a stunningly gorgeous woman in his arms.

And that he was reacting to her.

Gloria's eyes widened and for a second he thought she'd suddenly become aware that she had hurt something. But when she blurted a heartfelt, "I'm so sorry," followed by possibly the sexiest giggle he could ever recall hearing, Jack knew that there was nothing broken, bruised or injured.

At least where she was concerned. The jury was still out in regard to him.

Her eyes weren't on his face. Looking somewhat chagrined, she was staring at his chest. Jack looked down to see what she was looking at. The roller she'd been wielding was still clutched in her hand. He realized that Gloria must have accidentally hit him with it when she'd come sailing off the ladder. He was now sporting the same color across his chest that was on the freshly painted wall. Periwinkle blue.

He frowned. It didn't take much imagination to realize how narrowly she'd missed hitting his face. "I thought the idea was to paint the wall, not me."

"I'm so sorry," she repeated.

Looking closer, he could see that Gloria was obviously battling facial muscles, trying to keep them in line so that she could at least look somewhat contrite. But the grin was winning. Why he found that endearing rather than annoying he had no idea.

She blew out a breath, still tugging the corners of her mouth down. "Lucky thing I had you put on those coveralls."

"I think it was luckier that I was here to catch you."

"It was only one rung," she pointed out. "And I wouldn't have slipped if you hadn't made me so nervous."

Other than the incident with the air bag, Gloria Mendoza struck him as someone who possessed nerves of steel. And, he had to admit, he also found it a little intriguing.

His face still inches away from hers, Jack searched her expression for the telltale signs of humor. But this time, there was none. She was serious. His interest heightened.

"I make you nervous?"

Okay, so maybe she shouldn't have said that, Gloria upbraided herself. But it wasn't as if she were giving away some kind of deep, dark state secret. The man had to know that his looking over her shoulder was making her second-guess herself. That kind of thing would make anyone nervous.

Gloria looked at him pointedly. She decided not to backtrack. Honesty was usually the best policy, anyway. Lies were far harder to keep straight. "Yes, you do. By the way—" amusement played across her lips "—when do you think you'll be putting me down?"

He'd gotten so caught up in his reaction to her, he'd completely forgotten that he was still holding her. Feeling a little like an idiot, Jack set her on the floor. As he did so, it felt as if he was doing it in slow motion. He was utterly aware of every movement, every part of her body that came in contact with his as he released her.

Moreover, he could feel a reluctance humming in his body, an annoying reluctance he was entirely unfamiliar with.

Well, perhaps not entirely, he amended silently, but it had been a long, long time since he'd felt the stirrings of genuine desire awakening his body.

It was just a male reaction to a beautiful woman, he insisted, nothing more.

Except that he generally wasn't laid siege to by those kinds of feelings. He kept himself so busy that physical reactions were things that, for the most part, did not enter into his life. Even on those rare occasions when he had to take someone to a business function, he was more interested in working the room, in securing professional alliances for the bank, than he was with being attentive to his date of the evening.

He might be a brilliant strategist in the corporate world, but in the social realm, he knew that he was woefully out of step.

And he intended to remain that way no matter what the hell was going on here.

"How…" His throat felt strangely tight and he cleared it to not sacrifice his normal deep pitch. "How exactly do I make you nervous?"

When she raised her eyes to his, he felt something turn over in his belly then tighten into a knot. "Just knowing you're watching does it."

Jack fell back on sarcasm, his weapon of choice around someone like Gloria. "Can't very well walk around with a blindfold when I'm around you, can I?"

"No." Her mouth curved and he had the oddest desire to taste her lips. To see if they were as velvety smooth as they appeared.

The thought sent a jolt through his system.

What the hell was wrong with him? He was Jack Fortune, he could have any woman he wanted and he didn't want any.

He didn't want any, he underscored fiercely, knowing in his gut that he was doing one damn poor job of convincing himself.

For self-preservation, he took a step away from her. It made him angry that he suddenly seemed to have no control over himself. "Okay, where do you want me?" he snapped at her.

An answer flew to her lips. She counted herself fortunate that her mouth was closed at the time because what she would have said in response to his question would have gotten them both in trouble.

Next to me. In bed.

She was just as startled to think it as he would have been to hear it. What in heaven's name had come over her? After realizing just how bad Gary was for her, she had managed to wean herself off the idea of men altogether. They were in part responsible for the uneven, disastrous path she'd followed for more than ten years.

But her bet with her sisters had been more for their sakes than for her own. When she'd made it, she'd been more than confident that she wouldn't succumb to any kind of temptation because after what she'd been through with Gary and the men who had come before, she was utterly certain that she could swear them off as easily as a nonsmoker could swear off cigarettes.

So why did smoking suddenly seem so alluring?

The man didn't even like her, for heaven's sake. And he was the son of the man who was backing her business. This had "complications" stamped all over it. Was she utterly out of her mind?

Yes, she had to be. Because she didn't need or want to be involved with any men except for those within her own family. End of story.

Except that it wasn't. Damn him, Jack was holding her in place with that dark look in his eyes, the one that should be putting her back up because it generally appeared to be so superior-looking.

But her back wasn't up and she felt as if her body had been placed on alert. Waiting for something to happen. Dreading it and wanting it at the same time.

Her mouth felt dry. Gloria was uncomfortably aware that other more sensitive parts of her body had obviously absorbed all the moisture. She shifted her weight. It didn't help.

"Where do I want you?" she repeated, as if giving the matter genuine thought rather than lip service. She looked around the shop. There were only so many places for him to work. "Over there would be nice," she finally replied, pointing vaguely toward the opposite wall.

It was as far from her as was physically possible within the store. In distance there was safety. Or so she could hope.

"Okay," he agreed mechanically. He wasn't even looking where she was pointing.

Instead of picking up the paint can that Gloria had pushed up against the counter, Jack took the paint roller out of her hand and placed it on top of the closed container.

"You're not moving." The words, uttered in slow motion, tasted like cotton.

His eyes were intent on hers as he made up his mind. The second he did, excitement telegraphed itself through him. "I think that we need to get something out of our system first."

Her mind whirled as she desperately searched for something to say. Something flippant to put him off because, God help her, she had a feeling she knew what was coming. And that it would be her undoing.

She took a deep breath. "I was never one for purging."

"Sometimes—" his voice caressed her "—it has to be done in order to move forward."

Think, Glory, think. "I heard leeches are coming back into vogue."

Damn it. It felt as if his eyes were nailing her in place. This wasn't even sporting. Why couldn't Patrick Fortune have had ugly children? Or, barring that, why did he have to have a son who set her pulse racing the moment said son was anywhere within fifteen feet of her?

It just wasn't fair, she'd done her time, Gloria thought in mounting desperation, still not moving from where she stood. She didn't want to sink back into the velvet confines of desire. She wanted to be a nun—no, better than that, she wanted to be like one of those poor souls in Arabian fairy tales whose duty it was to guard the sultan's wives. Eunuchs had their desire made null and void.

There was nothing null and void about her reaction to him.

Damn, she was supposed to be through with desire.

Jack pretended to dig through his pockets, searching for imaginary leeches. "Fresh out."

"That's a shame." Gloria could feel the air getting caught in her throat. It had to be forced out. "I'll take a rain check."

"Gloria?"

Jack's breath whispered along her skin. She would have swallowed if only there was something to swallow. "Yes?"

"Shut up."

He saw a flash of temper in her eyes before it faded away. It only served to excite him further. Jack feathered his fingers through her hair, framing her face as he tilted it up to his.

If her heart hammered any harder, it was going to break into a million pieces. In self-defense, she began to talk again. "I heard a moving target is more of a challenge."

"All right then, consider me challenged."

He ran his thumb along her lower lip. He felt a pulsing in his loins as desire took a larger bite out of him. Unable to breathe, Jack brought his mouth down on hers.

Her mind went blank.

Her body went on automatic pilot.

Gloria threaded her arms around his neck, leaning her body into his as something that sounded vaguely like Handel's "Hallelujah Chorus" suddenly exploded inside her body and head.

Sunshine shot beams right and left, all but setting her on fire.

No, scratch that, she thought, *he* was setting her on fire.

Desperation scrambled through her, screaming, "Mayday." Damn it, it wasn't supposed to be like this.

But oh dear Lord, it was glorious.

She clung harder, kissed harder. Determined that if she was going to be plowed under, she was going to leave her mark on him before she disintegrated.

It wasn't working.

He'd made himself beard the lion in his den. Her den as the case was, he amended. More than anything, he wanted to get this, whatever it was that was bedeviling him, out of his system, put it behind him so that he would stop being ravaged by the claws of temptation and get on with his life.

In his experience, nothing ever lived up to hype, never came close to meeting expectations. Immeasurable disappointment always followed swiftly in the wake of anticipation, even minor anticipation. Forget about anything major. Major expectations always brought major disappointment crashing down about his ears.

And yet, he wasn't disappointed.

At least, not in his expectations. What he was disappointed in was himself. Because instead of backing away, instead of feeling nothing more stirring than a smattering of indifference when he kissed her, he wanted more.

Hell, he wanted her.

Here, now, with paint being transferred from his coveralls to hers, he wanted to make love with her on the floor, on the counter, against the ladder. Everywhere and anywhere.

A rush was traveling through him the likes of which he couldn't begin to fathom.

He wanted no part of it, it would only serve to confuse and complicate everything.

And yet he wanted more.

Wanted to embrace this sweet, agonizing sensation and fall into it until it completely cocooned him.

His very lungs ached.

It was not unlike the way they had felt when he had run his one and only New York marathon at the age of thirty. Any second now his lungs were going to explode. They'd already put him on notice.

With effort, he pulled himself back, abruptly ending what he'd abruptly started.

Gloria looked up at him, her expression as dazed as he felt.

It was a full minute before there was enough air in her lungs for her to form even a single word. "So," she finally whispered.

"So," he echoed, his mind nothing more than a vast wasteland.

Gloria pressed her lips together, wanting to kiss him again. Wanting to make love with him. Grateful that he hadn't pressed the advantage that was so obviously his. Eventually she gathered together enough breath to say, "It's behind us."

Not by a long shot, Jack thought, unless he exerted superhuman control. Still, for the sake of sanity he went along with the pretense.

"Guess so."

Any second now she was going to do something very stupid and throw herself back into his arms. Desperation began to vibrate through her. Her eyes never leaving his face, she took a step backward. "Maybe we should get back to work."

"Maybe."

All he could do was utter a solitary word, perhaps two. The way his thoughts were all scrambling into each other, he didn't think that he was capable of constructing a coherent compound sentence. Right now, every word in his vocabulary was on a fantastic ride inside the blender that was his brain, whirling around and making no sense whatsoever.

Her legs felt shaky, just the way they had when he'd pulled her out of the car earlier this week right after the air bag had threatened to separate her from her claim to being a rational being. Maybe she should lump him right up there with claustrophobia. Heaven knew he had the same kind of impact on her that she felt when she was confined to small spaces. Panic had been at the center of her reaction just now. The kind of panic that occurred when she found circumstances utterly out of control and beyond her reach.

He had done that to her.

So why did she want to kiss him again?

And why in heaven's name did she want to take what was going on here to the next level?

The second she'd thought of making love with him, something snapped to attention inside of her, an iron resolve set in place to keep her sane.

No, damn it, she wasn't going to go that route again, she wasn't going to follow her hormones down that same hazardous, slippery slope. She was older, wiser— well, at least older. Wasn't wisdom supposed to kick in at some point by now?

Willing herself back to some semblance of composure, she looked down at her overalls. The vivid splotch of paint she'd smeared across his chest when he had caught her had transferred itself onto her. Despite the seriousness of the situation she found herself in, Gloria could feel her mouth curving.

"Looks like we're part of some club." And then she cleared her throat, determined to give the performance of a lifetime. She fixed a bright, cheerful smile to her lips, the kind she summoned when dealing with a particularly trying customer whose account she wanted to acquire.

"Well, I'm glad that we got that out of our systems. Now maybe we can get down to work." She pointed toward the far wall. "If you take that wall over there, I'll finish up over here."

She sounded glib, as if she was accustomed to being kissed by men all the time.

Given the way she looked, maybe she was, Jack decided. Women like Gloria were the object of a great many men's fantasies and desires.

Something else stirred inside of him. Jealousy.

Jack banked it down, swiftly, firmly. There was no way he could be jealous. He hardly knew her. And it was going to stay that way.

He gratefully took his cue from the woman, relieved that she wasn't asking to have some kind of a heart-to-heart about what he had just foolishly done. A lot of other women would have demanded to have it out, asking him where he thought "this" was going to go.

As if he knew.

He hadn't a clue. He didn't even know what "this" was. And right now, he wasn't up to discussing anything except how many coats of paint she wanted to spread on her walls. Anything else would have required a more complex thinking process than he was capable of mustering at this point in time.

Nodding, he picked up the container of paint and took the roller she handed him. "Thanks."

Her throat felt bone-dry as she replied, "Don't mention it."

"I won't."

It was a promise he was making her, she suddenly realized.

She stood and watched him for a second as he pried off the container's lid, then poured some of the contents into a tray. Did that mean he had felt something, too? It would be nice to know that she hadn't been alone during the blitzkrieg she'd just experienced.

"Fine," she responded.

Then, to keep him from saying anything else, Gloria turned up the radio. A love song filled the air. She was quick to switch stations. But the next one belonged to a call-in talk show. The host was venting about a proposed tax bill. Muttering under her breath, she switched around until she found a country-and-western station.

With a smile, she left it on.

Roller raised to begin, Jack groaned as he looked at her over his shoulder. "Oh, God, you actually listen to country music?"

Good, they were back in their corners again, she thought. On opposite sides of an issue. She waited for the safe feeling to return, the one that told her she had nothing to fear.

This time, the feeling didn't come.

Maybe later, she thought hopefully. "Every chance I get."

Jack frowned, turning back to the wall. Trying to block out the music. "I didn't think you were the type for crying-in-your-beer songs."

"I'm not." She loved music and country and western was her favorite kind. "And they don't cry in their beer. There're a lot of good words, a lot of good sentiments to be garnered from country-and-western music."

"If you say so."

"Yes," she said cheerfully, dipping her roller in the tray, "I do."

She began to hum to the tune on the radio, doing her best to silence the tune her body was humming as she remembered that kiss.

Chapter Nine

There was a pizza between them on the back room desk. Because they'd badly needed a break after three hours of painting, Gloria had ordered a pepperoni pie from the pizzeria at the other end of the mall. Large, half-finished containers of soda stood like frosty sentries on either side of the opened box, standing guard over the more than half-consumed pie.

There was a great deal more than dough, cheese, sauce and pepperoni shimmering in the air between them, though.

Tasting a bit of sauce along her mouth, Gloria wiped her lips before continuing to work on her slice. She still didn't know what to make of Jack, or even if she should try.

But Jack Fortune wasn't the kind of man you could just write off or walk away from.

Especially after he'd kissed her in a manner that would have burned off a woman's socks.

Better just to go on eating and not say anything, Gloria told herself, even though the aftereffects of his kiss were lingering a lot longer than she'd thought they would.

That was only because she'd been celibate so long. Even plain tap water tasted like sparkling wine if your thirst had gone unquenched for two years.

Trouble was, she thought, watching Jack beneath hooded eyes, she hadn't realized she even *was* thirsty until she'd taken a sip.

Annoyed that she couldn't stop her mind from wandering down a path she didn't want it to go, she took a healthy swig of her diet soda and then leaned forward to take another slice of pizza.

At the same time that he did.

Both reaching into the box, their hands brushed against one another. It took effort not to pull back her hand. When he raised his eyes to hers, she said the first thing that popped into her head. "You lasted longer than I thought you would."

What the hell was that supposed to mean? Was she talking about his staying here after he'd kissed her? "Come again?"

"Painting," she explained, picking up her slice. "I half expected you to make a U-turn at the door when I suggested you put on the coveralls and pitch in." *And I*

would have stayed feeling a whole lot safer if you had,
she thought. "Thanks to you, we're almost done." She
flashed a grin, pausing to take a bite of what amounted
to her fourth slice. "At this rate, I'll be ready to open in
another week. The man who does the lettering is coming tomorrow." She watched as he took another slice
himself.

Jack raised a brow in mock surprise. "You mean,
you're not going to do that yourself, too?" Where was
she putting all this food? he wondered. So far, the
woman had consumed more than his last three dates put
together and she looked fantastic doing it.

Careful, buddy, he warned himself. *You're on dangerous ground here. You start admiring the way a
woman eats, you're lost.*

Gloria shook her head and laughed. "No way. I've
got terrible handwriting. No one would know what the
name of the store was."

He was vaguely aware of nodding in response, hardly
hearing what she was saying. His attention was riveted
to the way her mouth moved as she spoke. To the way she
breathed. Because it was warm inside, she'd unzipped her
coveralls down to her waist when she'd sat at the desk.
Beneath the bland garment with its paint splatters she was
wearing a tank top that adhered to her like a hot-pink skin.
It molded itself to her breasts, softly hinting at cleavage
while it brought out the deep black of her hair.

She'd loosened her hair, as well. It was skimming
along her back now like a black velvet cape.

One hand holding his slice, the other wrapped around the soda container, Jack could still feel an itch working itself across his palms.

He wanted to touch her. To run his palms along her body. He wanted to see for himself if it was as soft, as firm, as it appeared.

In a desperate attempt to mentally backpedal before he found himself in too deep, he searched for something to use as a barricade between them. Something official. "What kind of insurance are you going to be carrying?"

It took her a moment to absorb the question. He'd been looking at her with a gaze hot enough to burn away her coveralls and everything else, as well. She was grateful to talk about something as bland as insurance. Even so, she took a sip of the cold soda to quench a thirst that only partially resulted from the spicy slice of pizza she was consuming.

"Same as before," she told him. Then, in case he hadn't come across that when he was conducting his intrusive research into her life, she added, "I went with Gibraltar Insurance when I opened up my store in Denver." Before he could ask, she gave him the reasons behind her choice, enumerating them on her fingers. "Reasonable rates, accessible agents. They were right there for me after the robbery."

"Robbery?" The slice halfway to his lips, Jack stopped and looked at her incredulously. "You were robbed?"

Gloria bit her tongue, but it was too late. She should have done that *before* she'd said anything.

Big mistake, her mind taunted.

She shrugged as carelessly as she could, dismissing the incident, and then smiled at him prettily as she held up her thumb and forefinger barely three inches apart. "It was just a small robber."

"Bullets are the same size no matter how tall or short the shooter," he pointed out.

Damn, she wished she'd kept her mouth shut. "Yes," she said patiently, "I suppose they are. But no one was hurt," she was quick to add. "The guy who robbed us looked more scared than anything."

"You saw his face?"

"His eyes," Gloria corrected. "And he was terrified." She just *knew* he'd had to have been driven to do what he had by awful circumstances. "If my customer hadn't started hyperventilating just then, I think I might have had a shot at talking the robber out of what he was doing."

Just what kind of a nutcase was his father backing? The woman was certifiably insane. "Or a chance at getting shot—"

She finished off her piece and picked up a fresh napkin, wiping her fingers. "You know, Jack, you really have to do something about that upbeat outlook of yours."

There was nothing funny about the situation she was telling him. "I'm a realist."

Collecting a handful of used napkins from the desk, she dumped them into the garbage can, then cocked her head, studying him. "Maybe that's your problem."

He resented what she was implying. "I don't have a problem." *Other than dealing with you and these weird feelings.*

Gloria looked him in the eye, sensing that he was a soul in turmoil. More or less just the way she was right now.

"Are you happy?" she suddenly challenged.

Where the hell had that come from? "Ecstatic," he told her through clenched teeth.

Gloria laughed, the sound rippling through him like rings in a lake marking a disturbance. Which was exactly what the sound of her laughter created inside of him. One hell of a disturbance.

"All right, then maybe you don't have a problem," she allowed glibly.

"Thank you," he replied icily before getting back to the topic they were both pretending to discuss with interest. "What are you paying for insurance?"

One corner of her mouth rose in a teasing, provocative smile. "That's a little personal, don't you think?"

"A kiss is personal." Now why the hell had he said that? He'd promised himself not to think about or make reference to what had transpired earlier. The less time spent on that, the better. It was almost as if he was doomed to repeat it.

Jack quickly tried to distract her from his error. "This is business."

She gazed at him, all wide-eyed innocence. "Then you didn't mean business before?"

His eyes narrowed. "When?"

"When you kissed me?"

He stood by his original reason, no matter how flimsy and paper-thin it seemed. "I was just trying to get it out of the way."

"Oh. Yeah. Right," she murmured, the words emerging one at a time in slow motion. "Okay, then."

She quoted him the price she was paying. He looked at her in surprise.

"And that covers it?"

"Two million dollars' worth of coverage. I don't expect to have more than that on hand at any one time. Less, most likely. I provide a service," she explained. "Creating something to match the customer's personality rather than selling them something out of my inventory because I over-ordered sapphires last month."

It was an interesting philosophy, but he doubted its validity. "How can jewelry reflect a person's personality?" he scoffed.

She studied him for a long moment, then said, "Yours would be reflected in a gold ring. With a panther carved out of black onyx embossed on it. And maybe one small eye that seemed to watch you no matter where you moved. An emerald."

"Is that how you see me?" He wanted to know. "Flashy gold with embossed onyx?"

He was trying to throw her off. "Nothing flashy about gold," she informed him. "All the kings wanted it. And the ring would be in the image of a panther," she said pointedly. "That's how I see you. A panther. Sleek, deadly. Showing your opponents no mercy." *That* was the way she saw him, she insisted silently. Cold, removed.

Nothing cold about the way he kisses.

She banked down the stray thought. It had no place here.

Gloria forced a smile to her lips. "I've done a little homework on you, too." He looked surprised. And not pleased. "In the age of the Internet, no one's safe."

He dropped the last slice he'd been nursing back into the box. It was there alone. Between them they'd polished off almost an entire large pizza. "Apparently."

For some reason the space around her felt as if it was getting smaller, she realized. She could feel her claustrophobia kicking in. But for once, she almost embraced it. It allowed her to block out the other sensations that were swirling through her, the ones that worried her a great deal more than an attack of claustrophobia did. She knew how to deal with that: get out in the open again as fast as possible. Dealing with this attraction to Jack Fortune was another matter. And she wasn't going to be free of it until he went back to New York.

Rising, she brushed off her hands. "I'm going to go finish up," she announced.

Jack nodded, then looked back at the slice he'd just dropped. He picked it up again, using it as an excuse. He needed to regroup. "I'll be out in a minute."

She gave him a meaningful look. "Don't hurry."

Jack sat back in the straight-backed chair she'd rustled up, watching her walk out of the small office. Watching the way her hips moved from side to side like a lyrical song.

More like a prophecy of doom, he told himself. And he would do well to heed it.

Gloria knew she needed help.

If she hadn't been aware of it before, that kiss she'd allowed to happen—that kiss she'd more than wel-comed—had shown her just how vulnerable she was.

The man exuded sexuality with every breath he took. As they finished painting the showroom, she caught herself staring at Jack's coveralls a half a dozen times, wanting to take them off him using just her teeth.

Instead of getting better, this attraction was getting worse.

If she wasn't careful, she was going to wind up ex-actly where she had that time she'd come off a three-day bender after she'd had that awful falling out with Christina. When the fog had left from her brain, leav-ing behind one killer of a hangover, she'd discovered herself in bed with a man she hadn't recognized no matter how hard she'd tried to activate her brain.

She'd made a promise to herself then, a promise never to wind up beside a man she had no intention of being with again.

Gloria had an uneasy feeling that promise was going to ring hollow if she didn't do something to reinforce it, and fast.

She needed backup. She needed to touch base with someone sensible, someone who was grounded, who'd keep her grounded.

Until Jack had kissed her, she would have said that person was her. But after feeling lightning flashing wildly through her veins, she knew that she had just been kidding herself.

Just like alcoholics never really fully recover but remain one for the rest of their lives, the same could be said for a woman who made bad choices. She was doomed to remain in that mode, to continue making bad choices because she was constantly being drawn to men who were bad for her.

And in his own way, Jack Fortune was bad for her. He certainly didn't come with the promise of a happily-ever-after attached to him. Jack was clearly a man who wanted no attachments. Any sort of physical relationship she shared with him would be just that, physical, nothing more. It wouldn't lead anywhere. Besides, she'd had her share of hurt feelings and wasn't eager to go through that again.

To give the man his due, he hadn't pushed his advantage—and he'd definitely had one—when he'd kissed her. God knew she wasn't a pushover any longer, but with the right man—or the wrong one, depending on which side of the situation you were on—she had absolutely no willpower to speak of. Until he'd blown her resolve to pieces, she'd thought she had, but now she knew she didn't.

Which meant that she was going to have to be more vigilant, she told herself as she dipped her roller into an all but empty paint tray.

She could swear she felt him watching her.

That made her reinforce her promise to herself: no more being caught alone with him, even with paint buckets between them. If she was going to have any further dealings with Mr. Jack Fortune, there was going to have to be someone, anyone, present at the time.

But for now she needed to talk to someone rational, someone more cold-blooded and tougher than herself. Her sister Christina was the perfect choice.

Gloria put on the last finishing strokes, then retired her roller. Jack, she noticed, was still busy. She moved to the far end of the showroom—as far from Jack as she could get.

She knew she could turn to Sierra just as easily, but secretly she'd always admired her cool, calm, collected older sister. Even during the height of her rebellion and her awful period of acting out, a part of her had longed to be exactly like Christina.

The second she came home, Gloria shed her coat, purse and shoes and made a beeline for the telephone. Her body was still humming from this afternoon, from an onslaught of desire that almost had her kissing Jack as he took his leave. That had to stop.

Gloria reached for the phone and just as her fingers came in contact with the receiver, it rang beneath her hand. She hesitated, looking at her Caller ID. The number identified the call as coming from Fortune-Rockwell Bank. Jack?

The second she thought of him, her pulse rate escalated. God, this had to stop, she thought again.

She couldn't talk to him, she told herself. She'd let her answering machine pick up, then call Christina.

Gloria made her way to the kitchen, trying to ignore the phone, listening for the sound of a male voice anyway. What she needed, she decided, was a cup of coffee. Strong, black coffee. And maybe a lobotomy.

The machine beeped. She held her breath even as she told herself not to.

"Glory? It's just me, Tina, calling to see how you were doing. I'll try you again la—"

Pivoting on her stockinged heel, Gloria made a dive for the phone on the coffee table. She managed to lift the receiver just as her sister was about to hang up. "Tina? Are you there?"

"Yes, I'm here." Relieved, Gloria sank onto the sofa. Her legs felt as if they had all the structural integrity of thin rubber bands. "You sound breathless. What's up?"

If she was going to have a serious conversation with Christina, she wanted it to be face-to-face, not over the phone. So for now, she just went with the obvious excuse. "Just dashing across the room to get to the phone before you hung up."

"Didn't realize you were that eager to talk to me," Christina teased, then her voice grew tight with emotion. "I've missed you, Glory. Why did we waste so much time getting back together?"

"My fault." She was willing to take all the blame for the schism. She'd been the stubborn one, the one whose brain had been pickled more than half the time. "But it's over now. We're back in the same area and we're friends again. That's all that counts." She made herself comfortable, just as she had in the old days when she'd spend hours on the phone with nothing serious pressing on her conscience. "So, what's up?"

"That was what I was going to ask you," Christina responded, her voice warm, interested. "How's the place coming along?"

"Fantastic." She thought of the work she'd done last night. She'd stayed up until the wee hours, worked with a desktop publishing program. And then, for relaxation, she'd gotten in a little designing. "I've printed up all the fliers with the new address and posted them to all my old customers." Including one of the major studios that had commissioned her to design jewelry for one of its most popular situation comedies and the number one drama program on television. "I've even updated my Web site to let everyone know about the move and I've got a shipment of raw materials coming in at the end of the week."

"Raw materials," Christina echoed, then laughed. "First time I've ever heard diamond and emeralds called that. Sounds like you're getting ready to open sooner than you originally thought?"

"I am," Gloria confirmed. She tucked her feet under her and stared at the rain as it came down outside her window. It made the interior gloomy. "The weekend after this one."

"That soon?" She heard the soft sound of keys being struck on a keyboard. Christina was multitasking again. They got that from their parents, she thought. "I thought you said you hadn't decided on a painter yet?"

"I did. Me." And then she decided to be completely honest. "Along with some help."

"Help?" Her sister's voice sounded on alert.

Gloria took a deep breath, bracing herself before she continued. "Jack Fortune came by to harass me about insurance. He obviously didn't think I was bright enough to have any. I told him who my carrier was and I put him to work."

"Good girl." Delight resonated in Christina's voice as she applauded her.

Not exactly quite so good, Gloria thought, knowing she hadn't quite been truthful about the sequence of events. She glanced at her watch. It was too late today to meet Christina, plus she was pretty tired. The idea of a hot shower was too alluring to pass up. "Um, Tina, are you free for lunch tomorrow?"

"Sure, why?"

She paused for a second, then forged ahead. "I need to talk to someone."

"About Jack?"

At the last minute Gloria chickened out. She and

Christina had just gotten back on firm ground and she didn't want someone she admired, someone who had never made all the missteps that she had, to think of her as a weakling. At least, not before she could present her side of the picture.

"No," she denied vehemently. "I want to design a necklace for Mama and I thought I'd bounce a few ideas off you."

"Uh-huh."

Gloria's back stiffened. "Don't give me that big-sister, I-can-see-right-through-you stuff. I really want your opinion."

"Okay. Why don't you come by the office tomorrow and we'll grab a bite to eat while you impress me with your designs."

She grinned, pleased. She felt better already. "Sounds good. What time?"

"Make it eleven-thirty. I'll get off early so we can beat the crowd."

"You're on," Gloria said. "I'll see you tomorrow at eleven-thirty."

She was smiling as she hung up the receiver, all thoughts of Jack pushed aside. At least for the time being.

Chapter Ten

Preoccupied, Gloria didn't see Jack until she physically got on the elevator the next day.

She thought her radar would have warned her that the one person she desperately wanted to avoid was in the area. But just as she'd rounded the side that led to the bank she'd heard the bell sound for an arriving elevator car and, in a hurry to get the ride to the thirtieth floor in a cylindrical tube over with, she made a dash for it.

And narrowly avoided colliding with the tall, well-built man coming in from the other side.

Face to cloth, Gloria recognized the cut of the suit first. Custom. Hand-sewn. The cologne was a close second. There was no one else in the elevator to share the ride with them.

Her heart froze just as the doors closed behind her. She took a step back and looked up at him. Her verbal skills lagged behind by a full beat.

"Jack."

"Gloria." He acknowledged her presence a bit curtly. But she was the last person he wanted to run into, literally or otherwise. He was on his way to a private meeting with his father about the Gloria situation. After that little incident in the shop, for which he wholeheartedly accepted the blame, he definitely wanted out. According to her own words, her shop would be ready for business within the week. Her insurance was in order, as was her inventory. And she had a security firm coming out to safeguard the store against break-ins. There was no reason for him to stick around. He wasn't aware of the bank holding anyone else's hand so tightly.

His eyes washed over her. She was bundled up in a three-quarter-length suede coat. Suede had never been a turn-on for him.

Until now.

Maybe he should have arranged to meet his father for dinner instead, he thought darkly. There was precious little chance of her turning up at his father's house.

Damn it, why did she feel like a cross between a James Bond martini and a malt every time she ran into him? Stirred *and* shaken.

Gloria forced a smile to her lips. "Looks like we can't seem to avoid running into one another."

He decided that his best bet was to stare straight ahead at the steel doors. "Looks like."

As talkative as ever, she thought. Maybe she should have been grateful for that, but she wasn't. She hated silence when she was uncomfortable and right now after yesterday she was very uncomfortable.

What was he thinking? Had he relived that kiss over and over again the way she had? Or did he regret the impulse that had prompted him to turn her knees into churned butter?

Or had the whole thing been so insignificant he wasn't wasting any time at all thinking about it?

Gloria cleared her throat, summoning words to fill the silence. "I'm on my way to meet my sister for lunch. Christina," she added for good measure in case he had forgotten which sister worked here. When he made no effort to respond, she pressed, "You?"

A trace of confusion marred his perfect forehead. "Me, what?"

Was he tuning her out completely? "Who are you going to see?"

Jack turned his face forward again. "My father." *To get me off this damn assignment from hell once and for all.*

"Oh." Extracting words out of the man was like trying to pick hot coals out of a fireplace. They came swiftly, but sparingly. "Tell him I said hi."

Jack made no reply, merely nodding that he'd heard

her. According to the flashing numbers at the front of the car, the floors were flying by.

Not fast enough to suit him, he thought. The space within the smooth, steel-gray walls was filling up with her perfume and it was getting to him. Arousing him. Making him remember what her lips had felt like pressed against his.

Ten more flights to go.

And then the elevator jerked to a stop. The light went out, leaving them in complete darkness.

The next moment he felt his arm being clutched. "Clawed at" was more like it.

"What just happened?"

Her voice was breathless, panicky. Just like when the truck had struck his car flying through the intersection. "It's just a malfunction. Don't start screaming," he warned.

He thought he heard her swallow. "I won't." She sounded utterly unsure of her promise.

"It'll only be a few seconds," he assured her. This was a relatively new building. Fortune-Rockwell had moved out of its old home office into this one less than five years ago. Everything was supposed to be state-of-the-art.

Which meant that these kinds of things weren't supposed to happen.

"The lights are bound to come back on."

Extricating his arm, he put his hands out to feel for the wall in an attempt to find the phone. Somehow he got turned around and he found her instead.

Instantly he pulled back his hands. Whatever he

had touched—and he had a real suspicion what that had been—was incredibly soft, even if it was packaged in suede.

"Sorry," he muttered.

"It's okay."

Her reply was barely above a whisper. He could hear the fear mounting in her voice. "We're going to be all right," he told her firmly.

"I know we are."

Although she didn't sound quite so sure she believed him.

Just as he wondered if she was going to faint, an auxiliary light came on. The illumination it cast was dim, but at least they were no longer in the dark.

Her skin looked almost translucent, he thought, glancing at her face. "There." Jack indicated the emergency light source. "See?"

"Yes," she whispered. "I can." She could see just how small, how confining, the space was. For some reason the dim light only made it feel that much smaller. A tightness was taking hold within her chest.

"And so can I," he told her. And what he saw was unadulterated fear. The same fear that had been in her eyes when he'd pulled her out of the car when the air bag had deployed. "It's going to be all right," he repeated. The words felt empty, hollow, highlighting the frustration he felt.

She turned desperate eyes on him. "When? When is it going to be all right?"

"As soon as the lights come back on."

He knew his answer wasn't very reassuring. Nothing frustrated him more than not having control over a situation. Annoyance strumming through him, he opened the panel just above the keypad of floor buttons and extracted the closed-circuit telephone receiver. "Hello? Hello? Is anyone there?"

There was no answer. For a minute he felt like hitting the receiver against the wall, but losing his temper wasn't going to solve their dilemma. He tried his cell phone. There was no signal. When it rained, it poured.

"The power must be out." Gloria's voice was hardly above a whisper. She could feel her throat closing up again.

He shook his head. "The phone lines are on a separate circuit." Swallowing a curse, he hung up the receiver. "Maybe some of the other elevators are out, too, and whoever is supposed to be answering the phone is out checking on another car."

"Yeah, right."

His attention shifted toward her. Poor lighting or not, she really didn't look too good. "Sit down before you fall down."

But Gloria remained standing where she was, her whole body as rigid as if it had been chiseled out of rock. She turned her eyes to his face.

This was what they meant by a deer-caught-in-the-headlights look, he thought.

"Do something." It was half a command, half an appeal.

Just what did she expect him to do? There were precious few options available. "Well, I'd get out and push the car up to the next landing, but my cape's at the cleaners."

"Do something," she repeated, more insistently this time.

Okay, he'd bite. "And just exactly what is it that you'd have me do?"

She shrugged helplessly. If she knew, she'd have done it herself. "I don't know—a guy thing." Looking around, she saw what appeared to be a removable panel directly above their heads. "Like climbing up and pushing that off."

He looked up at the same panel. "What good will that do?"

"We could climb out." With a dismissive snort, he looked down at her high heels. "I'm very nimble," she insisted.

He decided to humor her for the space of a moment. "Okay, supposing we could climb out, then what?"

She didn't know about him, but it would do her a world of good. "At least we wouldn't be trapped in here, suffocating."

"We're not suffocating. There's plenty of air in here."

She had her hand on his arm again. For a relatively small woman, she had really strong fingers. "Please."

Jack knew she wouldn't give up until he gave in. He

supposed that since there was no one answering him on the phone, it wouldn't hurt to try to see what was going on, although he wasn't about to attempt shimmying up the cables to the next floor. There was no way he could possibly pry open the doors on the next landing. Even if he were a weight lifter, it wouldn't be possible.

He moved to the wall and tested the integrity of the railing that ran along three sides of the car. Recessed from the wall, it seemed sturdy enough to hold him.

Jack glanced back at her. She'd shed her coat in a heap on the floor. "Come here, give me your shoulder."

He watched her tongue lightly run along the outline of her mouth and tried not to let it affect him. "Why?"

Exasperated by the situation and by the fact that there didn't seem to be anything he could do to negate the mounting anxiety in her eyes, he snapped, "Because I didn't have any breakfast this morning and I'm hungry." Taking her arm, he pulled her over to the wall. "I need it for leverage, that's why."

Removing his shoes, Jack clamped his hand on her shoulder. She wobbled a little, then braced herself. The phrase "iron butterfly" teased his brain. "You're sturdier than you look."

"So they tell me."

He raised his foot as far up as he could, getting it onto the railing. Gloria spread her legs apart, taking a stance as he pushed off her shoulder and rose up parallel to the wall. There was a space between the ceiling and where the sides ended. He secured his fingers along that ridge.

Moving in half inches, he managed to make it to the trapped door.

Holding on with one hand, he pushed the panel with the other. It took a little doing, but the panel finally gave way. Jack moved it to the side. Clearing an opening large enough to accommodate him, he pulled himself up with his arms.

Watching his every move, Gloria held her breath. She saw him disappear through the opening. For a moment she was alone. Alone in a small space. Just as she had been all those years ago. Perspiration was forming all up and down her spine. She could feel her blouse adhering to her back.

Damn it, stop panicking. It's not going to do you any good, she insisted silently.

Gloria forced her feet to move until she was standing directly under the opening that the panel had covered. She craned her neck. There was nothing but darkness outside the car.

"What do you see?"

"Nothing."

"Nothing?" Disappointment resonated through her like a death knell.

"Nothing," he repeated. "No lights, not even slivers of light between the floors. No nothing." Which, as far as he could see, could mean only one thing. "It looks like there's some kind of power failure going on in the building."

Her breath felt almost jagged as it caught in her throat. "Do you think it's affected the whole city?"

"Probably just us," he told her in the calmest voice he could muster.

And then he looked down into the car. She'd been right. He had to do something. "Look, I'm going to try to see if I can get to the next floor."

"No!" Her sudden cry surprised him. Her next words surprised him even more. "Don't leave me."

She wasn't being rational. "Gloria, I—"

"Don't leave me," she repeated, the urgency in her voice growing.

He supposed there was no way of knowing just how far up he was going to have to climb before he could get out. And if he left her, there was no telling what condition she'd been in by the time he could get back to her. He made his decision.

"Okay, stand back," he ordered. "I'm coming down."

She moved to the opposite wall, pressing her back up against it, her eyes never leaving his face. Gloria held her breath as she watched him jump down. He winced as he landed.

"Are you all right?"

He'd landed wrong on his ankle. Testing it now, he shrugged. "I'll live." And then he looked at his clothes. "But I don't know about my suit."

She tried to smile and succeeded only marginally. The space around her was growing smaller. "Can't stay clean around me, can you?"

"Doesn't look like it." They both jumped when the elevator phone rang. Jack grabbed it. "Hello?"

"Hello? This car number seven?" a deep male voice rumbled against his ear, carrying beyond the receiver.

Jack glanced up at the certificate housed behind glass. It okayed the car for service. He squinted to make out the number.

"Yeah. We're stuck."

"So are all the other elevator cars." The technician sounded harried and resigned at the same time. "Power's out throughout the building. You're going to have to hang tight."

Gloria was directly behind him. Desperate, she grabbed the phone from his hand and yelled, "How long?"

"Dunno. We're working as fast as we can." There was a pause, as if the technician was calculating time. "Couple of hours, maybe more."

"A couple of hours?" Her eyes widened as her claustrophobia threatened to take over every square inch of her. She could feel it cutting off her air, making her want to gasp.

"Can't be helped," the technician informed her.

Jack looked at her as she handed him the phone. "Is the blackout confined just to this building?"

"Looks more like a few blocks. As close as I can tell, a grid went out." Then, because nothing could be solved on the phone like this, the technician said, "I'll get back to you."

And suddenly the line went dead.

A fresh assault of panic struck Gloria. She felt as if they'd been abandoned.

"No, wait, wait," Gloria cried as she grabbed the receiver from Jack. But there was no one on the other end to hear her.

They were alone, she thought, anxiety coarsely rubbing against her. Alone for who knew how long?

Very gently, Jack pried the receiver out of her hand. The woman had a death grip, he thought as he removed her fingers from the phone and hung up.

The annoyance he'd initially felt had turned to protectiveness. "He'll call back when he has something to say."

Lips pressed together, she nodded. But when she spoke, there was despair in Gloria's voice. "We might be dead by then."

Maybe he could kid her out of it, he thought. "You always exaggerate like that?"

Instead of answering him, she turned desperate eyes up to his face. "Talk to me."

"I thought I was."

But she shook her head. "No, *talk* to me. Get my mind off this."

Maybe if he could get her to talk about her fears, it would help her to deal with the situation. "What is it with you and tight places?"

Ordinarily she might have said something flippant, or even denied that there was a problem the way he was implying. But the man had eyes. He could see there was a problem. Could hear it, too. There was no disguising her reaction, no matter how hard she tried. "I don't like them."

He laughed shortly. "That's rather obvious. Any particular reason?"

Instead of answering him immediately, Gloria took off her jacket, tossing it on top of her coat. She opened the top two buttons of her blouse. Even in this light, he could see the perspiration along her forehead and on her cheeks. It wasn't that hot in here, he thought.

Jack watched in fascination as she pulled her blouse out from the waistband of her skirt, fanning her middle with the shirttails.

When she paused and raised her eyes to his, he said, "Don't stop on my account."

She hated the feeling of desperation that was eating her alive. She should have outgrown it by now, risen above it. "It's hot in here."

It wasn't the heat she was feeling and they both knew it, but he let her have her lie.

"And panicking is going to make it seem hotter." He waited for a second, certain she would continue. But she didn't. That alone told him that the situation was dire. The woman never missed a chance to talk. "You didn't answer my question. Any particular reason confined spaces make you break out in a sweat?"

"Yes."

They weren't making any progress. "And that would be?"

Gloria's eyes shifted from his face. This wasn't something she talked about, at least not to anyone outside of her own family and even that was rare.

She glanced toward Jack. He was still waiting. Okay, maybe he deserved to know why she'd clawed his arm. At the very least, it would pass the time.

She took as deep a breath of the increasingly hotter air as she could and began.

"When I was a little girl, my family lived in Red Rock. My parents still live there." A slight smile faintly crossed her lips. "It was as developed then as it sounds." For just an infinitesimal second, she was that little girl again, free of the demons she had acquired. "Wonderful place to grow up," she testified. "My brothers and sisters and I had no end of places to play."

And then her expression sobered. "There was this one field that ran behind an abandoned old house. We used to call the house the Spooky place—"

"Very original," Jack commented, never taking his eyes off her. Watching emotions cross her face in the dim light.

"We were kids," she reminded him. And then, as he continued to watch her, she seemed to brace herself before she went on. "One day, we were playing hide-and-seek." Her breath began to grown audibly shorter. "The way we had a hundred times before."

She was going to stop. He saw it in her eyes. "And?" Jack prodded.

Gloria raised her chin, a shaky defiance trying to take hold. And failing.

"And I fell into this abandoned shaft. I found out later that it was an old well that had gone dry."

Suddenly she was there again, in that hole. The dirt walls threatening to close in on her with every grain of dust that fell. Tears rose to her eyes as she remembered the terror that had gripped her.

"Christina ran for help while my brothers and Sierra talked to me, trying to keep me calm. Christina came back with my mother who'd called the fire department. More and more people kept coming, blocking out the light. It took what felt like forever for them to get me out. I was six at the time," she whispered, more to herself than to him, "and convinced that I was going to die."

Gloria caught her lower lip between her teeth as she looked up at him again. "I stopped being fearless that day."

Chapter Eleven

Jack remained quiet as she talked, studying her. He could see that she was reliving the incident with every word she uttered.

He couldn't imagine experiencing that kind of overwhelming fear. He strode through places—small, large, beneath buildings and on the top-floor balcony of a New York skyscraper—without any thought of harm coming his way, knowing nothing would spring out to trigger an attack.

Are you really that different? a small voice whispered, coming out of nowhere to mock him.

Granted, places didn't scare him. But the thought of risking his heart, of somehow winding up again in that dark, empty abyss without the one he loved, scared the hell out of him.

Imprisoned him just as her fears imprisoned her.

Maybe they weren't that different, after all. Compassion washed over him.

"They'll be here soon," he promised again, this time more softly.

She looked up at him with eyes that belonged to the child she had been.

"No, they won't." Her voice was hardly above a whisper. She was struggling again to keep the hysteria at bay. To keep a tight lock on the panic that was scraping jagged nails inside of her, trying to break free. "If the whole building is out, it's going to take them a long time to get here in order to help us."

Breathe, Glory. Damn it, breathe. Nice and slow and steady. In, out. You know how to breathe, don't you?

Eyes wide, Gloria looked at the four walls surrounding her. She felt as though they were closing in.

She forced air into her lungs, praying she wouldn't embarrass herself in front of Jack.

Too late.

"I know I'm an adult," she began slowly, as if trying to lay down a foundation for herself, something steady for her to build on. Even as she did so, a feeling of futility began to take hold. "That this is all in my head. But I just can't…I can't…"

He took her hand in his, catching her before she

could verbally and mentally take off to places neither of them wanted her to go. "Tell me about yourself."

The abrupt order caught her off guard. She blinked. "What?"

"Tell me about yourself," he insisted. Male-female communication had somehow slipped beyond his realm. He tried to remember conversations he'd had with Ann when they were just getting to know one another. "Did you go to the prom in high school? Try out for the cheerleading squad?"

Stunned, Gloria stared at him as though he'd lost his mind. And then he heard a gratifying sound. Despite the pinched look between her brow, she began to laugh.

Jack couldn't remember when he'd heard a lovelier sound.

"Do I look like the cheerleader type to you?" she asked incredulously.

"I'm not sure." As he spoke, he found himself running his fingers through her hair. It felt incredibly silky to the touch, which was probably how the rest of her felt, too. "All I know is that you look like the kind of girl everyone in school would have noticed."

"They did." Gloria sighed, suddenly weary beyond words. She closed her eyes for a moment. But the next second, they flew open again, as though afraid that if she didn't keep vigil, the walls would rush up around her and flatten her. "But for the wrong reasons."

When he looked at her quizzically, she realized that she was going to have to elaborate. *You opened the door, now you have to step through.* "I was desperate to block out my fears. Claustrophobia, among other things." She let the phrase hang for a moment, more than a little reluctant to go into any detail.

He thought that Gloria had finished when she suddenly said with a careless shrug, "Some people are nasty drunks. I was a happy one."

The word "drunk" made something tighten within his chest. He remembered Ann. Remembered the way she'd giggle when tipsy. Looking back, it seemed to him that she was almost always giggling at the end.

"You drank?" He looked at her with new eyes as alarms went off in his head.

Too busy looking inward, Gloria missed the edgy look in his eyes. She nodded.

"I drank an ocean of alcohol, trying to drown my insecurities. But all that drinking did for me was give me another problem," she confessed. "Took me a long time to come to terms with that."

"You don't drink anymore?" There was skepticism in his voice. Ann had pretended to be "cured," too. More than once. And each time, he'd believed the lie. Hoping it was the truth.

"Nothing that'll give me a buzz. These days, my drink of choice is diet soda or sparkling nonalcoholic cider, nothing strong." She wasn't going to allow herself to fall into that trap again. "Hitting bottom made me want to surface again, to breathe fresh air." She looked around the dim interior. The walls *had* grown closer together. Her blouse was sticking to her body. She opened another button, but that didn't do anything to help. Just reminded her of how powerless she was at trying to control the situation. "Kind of what I want to do now."

Taking her chin in his hand, he moved her head until her eyes were level with his. She was sinking, he could see it. Jack banished the feelings that threatened to take over. Her drinking wasn't the issue here. Keeping her from succumbing to terror was.

"Keep talking," he ordered.

Heat and fear combined to make her irrational. "Why, so you can gather ammunition against me to take to your father?"

For a moment a scowl returned to his face. He reined in his temper. Maybe arguing with her could make her forget how she felt about being confined in the elevator. "Is that what you actually think of me? That I'm some kind of a snitch who goes behind people's backs?"

She wiped the back of her sleeve against her forehead. There was no air. No air. Frantic thoughts assailed her from all sides. She was going to melt. The cable was going to snap and they were going to fall twenty stories. She desperately tried to keep her mind on the conversation. "Going behind my back would imply secrecy. You've made no secret of how you feel about me."

He wanted to keep her talking at all costs. If she focused her anger on him, she might not think about being trapped. "And what's that?"

She blew out an annoyed breath, as if she was tired of playing games. "That you feel you've been saddled with something, someone beneath you."

His eyes held hers for a moment. No, not beneath him, he thought. The woman was clearly his match in every way. Maybe that was what he had against her. "Your intuitive skills aren't as sharp as you think they are."

"Oh?" Just then, she heard what she took to be the cables, creaking. They *were* going to fall down the shaft. Her throat closed so tightly she was afraid she was going to asphyxiate.

She clutched at his arm, staring up at the ceiling. "What was that?"

"Maybe the power trying to come back on," he lied. He was beginning to feel a little uneasy himself, but not because of the small space. His unease came from having her so close to him. From the fact that she seemed to fill up every space with her essence.

Her breathing was audible now. "Or the cables about to snap."

"Not going to happen," he assured her. "There's emergency equipment that comes on as an auxiliary fail-safe measure." He searched for a way to explain what he was saying so that it would penetrate the fog of fear crowding her brain. "Each floor has what amounts to brakes that come out and stop the car from plunging down to the ground floor."

She didn't look as if she believed him. Maybe she

had already gone into shock, he thought. What the hell were you supposed to do with a person in shock? Keep them moving? Have them lie down?

He decided to compromise. Jack slipped his arm around her shoulders. "Sit down," he instructed quietly. "Take a deep breath and hold it."

But she shook her head, her hair flying from side to side. "I can't. My lungs feel like they're going to explode."

If she kept on breathing like that, she was going to hyperventilate. He couldn't let that happen. Desperate for a solution, he let his instincts take over. Instincts born of inspiration, of need and, perhaps, of more than a touch of desire.

Jack brought his mouth down to hers.

At first she struggled against him, not because she didn't want to kiss Jack but because she couldn't get enough air into her lungs.

But then her breathing began to regulate itself as the center of her attention slowly shifted from the very real fear that, despite his assurances about the emergency fail-safes that had been put in when the elevators were installed, they were going to fall to their deaths, crushed inside a silvery coffin.

Instead, her focus turned to the kiss that was swiftly setting fire to the very blood in her veins.

Panic abated in increments.

Gloria felt herself being pressed against him, felt the length of his body imprint itself onto hers. Felt her response as desire, hidden behind thin bamboo walls, broke through, seizing her. Making her tighten her arms around him.

Her heart was pounding, but for an entirely different reason than before.

He'd meant only to divert her. To keep her from hyperventilating. He hadn't meant to get caught up in what amounted to an unorthodox first-aid application. Not like this. To make matters worse, she'd just shared something with him that had brought back memories he didn't want to deal with, that made him relive Ann's last days.

Maybe that was it. Maybe that had made him vulnerable.

And maybe it was none of the above. Maybe it just had to do with the woman in his arms. The woman he'd had an underlying yearning for since the first moment she had looked up at him with those incredible soft-brown eyes, turning his stomach to jelly and nearly turning his mind to mincemeat.

Kissing her only made him want her with a fierceness that was every bit as overwhelming as the claustrophobia he knew she was wrestling with.

Suddenly he realized that he had to step back, had to get air himself. Logic demanded that he try to clear his head.

But he didn't want to.

Didn't want to give up this wild surge that was pulsating through him, forging a path through his body. Making him aware of himself as a man.

He hadn't wanted, truly wanted, a woman since Ann had died, leaving him to wander emotionally isolated in this world. Oh, there had been biological needs since then, but he could always separate himself from them, step outside his body and watch as he went through the physical motions of having sex, his mind absent from the process.

Right now his mind was in full attendance and there was no separating anything. The logic that always presided over his life had somehow gotten lost.

Nothing mattered except that he wanted to make love with Gloria. Wanted to get lost within her as they kept the world at arm's length.

This wasn't like her, not anymore, Gloria kept telling herself. She didn't do things like this anymore: give up who and what she was with an abandonment that was so swift it all but jarred her very teeth. But all those encounters that had taken place in her past had been governed by inebriation. Her brain had always been liberally soused, the ability to think lost inside of a bottle.

But not this time.

She was stone-cold sober, drunk only on this sensation that was vibrating through her like the strings of a harp that had been plucked. She was drunk, but only on the idea of making love.

When his hands caressed her, Gloria moaned audibly, wanting him to touch her everywhere. To both soothe and stoke the fire that his nearness had created.

Gloria sucked in her breath. She felt his wide, capable hands delving beneath the blouse she'd pulled free earlier.

"You're trembling," he whispered, his breath warm on her neck.

He was going to pull away. She could feel it. She couldn't let that happen. Without admitting it, she knew where this was going. Needed this to go there. Needed him to make love with her.

"This isn't the time to withdraw," she breathed, pressing harder against him.

Jack felt completely, hopelessly, lost. The willpower he thought was second nature had somehow turned into so much sawdust. If she'd backed away, cried, asked him to stop, then maybe the willpower he'd treasured could have been resurrected. But every indication she gave him was that she wanted this as badly as he did.

He hadn't the strength to back away, to leave her of his own accord.

Still, he watched her eyes in the dim light for signs of fear, or mounting panic that had to do not with the enclosed space, but with what was happening.

Instead of fear, he saw desire.

Desire that mirrored exactly what was going on inside of him. He knew this was wrong. Clear-thinking adults didn't make love suspended above the twentieth floor of a skyscraper that had been pitched into darkness. *He* didn't make love like this. Mindlessly, and with complete abandonment.

Hell, he hadn't made love since Ann died. He'd had

sex. And each time had left him completely unsatisfied. Not wanting more, just wanting something. Something that wasn't there.

Something that whispered to him now. Making every fiber within his body yearn.

With swift, sure movements, Jack pulled her blouse away from her shoulders, pressed his lips to every inch of her soft flesh as it was exposed. His own breathing became as labored as hers.

His fingers worked the clasp that held her bra in place.

When she shivered against him as the lacy material fell away, he felt a volley of passion being fired through him that all but turned his body rigid with desire. He slid the button holding her skirt together out of its hole, then pulled it from her.

The dimness caressed her like a familiar lover. His gaze passed over her. Gloria was wearing nothing but heels and underwear. His stomach pressed itself against his spine.

Gloria could feel anticipation vibrating throughout her whole body, priming her for the final moment that she both craved and wanted to hold at bay so that she could savor the approach of the final moment. It felt as if her whole body was humming.

She forced her breathing to grow steadier, as if that would somehow keep her hands from shaking as she swiftly yanked his custom-made jacket and pants off of him.

It didn't.

Anticipation vibrated through her.

Like a person caught in a dream, Gloria could hardly remember unbuttoning his shirt. All she knew was that she wanted to press her fingertips along the hard ridges of his chest, wanted to leave imprints of his firm flesh on hers.

Wanted to be with him in the most intimate of covenants between a man and a woman.

Her mouth sealed to his, her fingers questing, smoothing, she felt him reacting to her. Heard his breathing grow more shallow. A thrill shivered through her as the extent of her power registered. He was hers. For a single shining moment in time, he was hers.

His hands were hot on her body. They sank to the floor of the elevator, cushioned by the clothes they had discarded.

One movement inviting, flowering into another.

She could feel every pulse point in her body responding to him. His mouth roamed over her chin, her throat, along the planes above her breasts. The hollow of her belly.

Everywhere he touched, he conquered.

She'd never wanted to make love with anyone the way she wanted to make love with Jack. All the nights she had spent with her husband combined hadn't equaled this single instance with Jack.

Maybe this was what had been missing from her marriage all along, mind-bending lovemaking. She'd married Gary because he'd been the first half-decent man she'd come across. She'd thought marriage to him would keep her safe. It hadn't.

This wasn't safe, either, but the risk was enticing, thrilling.

She felt a wild explosion rapidly moving forward through her system as, time and again, Jack brought her so very close to the edge, then withdrew so that she slid back.

Hot, moist kisses burned along her torso. Gloria twisted into them, wanting more. Wanting that final moment.

"Hurry," she whispered urgently against his ear, biting down on her tongue before she could add, "please." She wasn't going to beg, wasn't going to be pathetic, but oh, how he made her want.

Needs slamming through him, Jack stretched his body over hers, needing the contact. He refrained from entering, wanting to prolong this even though somewhere in the back of his mind, where reality still dwelled beneath a dark curtain, he knew they ran the risk of being discovered.

Was that adding to the thrill?

He didn't know. Didn't know anything at all anymore. Except that he had utterly lost himself.

When she raised her hips urgently against his, that was the last straw, the last enticement. Unable to hold back any longer, Jack entered her.

The rhythm was instantaneous, as if guided by something that was completely outside of him, something he had no control over.

The dance began sweetly, moving, growing in ever-increasing tempo. They tumbled around on the floor, moving from side to side, first with him on top, then her, then him again. With each movement, the urgency increased, growing more erratic, more demanding.

He was vaguely aware that he heard something breaking. Glass? But that wasn't possible.

The very air from his lungs began departing. He felt his mind swirling somewhere just out of reach as he pulled her closer to him, his arms tightening around her as if she was the most precious thing he had ever encountered.

Perhaps she was.

The climax was so powerful, it stole the last drop of his breath away.

He could feel his heart pounding so hard, it threatened to break out of his chest. Or was that her heart, pounding so hard against his?

He had no idea where he stopped and she began. They were like one. If he could, he would have remained like this, feeling himself inside of her. Feeling himself whole for the first time since his world had abruptly ended with the screech of tires and metal groaning against metal.

Listening, he could have sworn he heard that sound now. Metal, creaking, groaning. Somehow, in his brain, the past had merged with the present.

Then, abruptly, he felt Gloria's soft body turn rigid beneath him. A moment later her hands were pulling at him urgently. With effort, he pivoted himself up on his elbows to look down into her face.

Was she afraid again?

"The elevator," she cried.

"It's all right," he told her. "We're not going to fall." *Except, maybe he was.* The thought bounced at him out of nowhere.

But she was pushing him from her. "No," she cried, desperate to make him understand what she was trying to say. "We're not falling, we're going up!"

Just then, the lights went on.

Chapter Twelve

The realization penetrated. In a few seconds they were not going to be alone anymore.

The next moment they were quickly scrambling into their clothes, desperate to get dressed before the elevator was brought up to the next working level, which was only five floors up.

Gloria didn't even take time to breathe. Her heart was racing almost as madly as it had been when they'd been making love. But this time her fingers felt not only clumsy but fat, as if they didn't even belong to her. It made closing her buttons annoyingly difficult. She didn't even bother to tuck in her blouse. There wasn't time.

Wasn't time to even notice how magnificent his body

was as he slid his trousers back on. But somehow, she managed.

Gloria felt her body start to tingle all over again.

It wasn't until she had on her skirt and blouse that she realized she'd forgotten to put on her underwear. The lacy panties were next to Jack's foot. But as she reached for them, the doors began to open. Her heart slammed hard against her chest.

There wasn't going to be time to put her underwear on. Worse, whoever had come to rescue them would see them right there out in plain view.

Seeing her dilemma, Jack quickly scooped up the errant underwear and shoved them into his pants' pocket. He ran his hand through his hair just as a technician peered in. He was half a floor above them. The elevator wasn't level with the landing.

"Sorry," the man apologized, raising his wide shoulders in a depreciating shrug. "'Fraid this is the best we can do right now."

Gloria didn't care that the top of her head was level with the barrel-chested man's kneecap. The psychological rush of new air was wonderful and she savored it as she dragged it into her lungs.

At the same time she felt the oddest sting of disappointment. The interlude between them was over.

A swirl of emotions danced through her, each jockeying for lead position. Sorrow, need, happiness, relief and a dozen more. She shut them all away. She just wasn't up to sorting through her half-formed feelings right now.

Maybe you never will, a small voice whispered. She'd found that avoiding things was better than letting them eat away at her.

She focused on their rescuer; a short, squat man wearing navy-blue coveralls. It was safer that way.

"Don't be sorry," she told him breathlessly. "At least you got the elevators running again."

He beamed at her even as he shook his partially bald head. "Wasn't me. The power company gets all the credit. They got the juice flowing again. Rumor says it was some squirrel biting through a line that did it."

Jack moved her jacket and purse aside and stood behind her. He saw her shoulders suddenly grow rigid. What was she afraid of? They were getting out. "I'll give you a boost," he volunteered, then glanced up at the other man. "I'll hand her off to you."

Gloria watched the technician brace himself as he got down on one knee. His arms were stretched out, readying to take hold of hers and pull her out. A feeling of déjà vu washed over her and she shivered. This was just like when she'd been stuck in the well. With one very notable exception.

Suddenly she felt Jack's hands taking hold of her waist. The next second he was raising her toward the technician as if she were nothing more than a life-size doll.

The pressure and warmth of his palms surged all through her. Stirring her. She was almost sorry that the power had come back on again.

Almost.

Before she could dwell on the sensation, the technician took hold of her hands and began pulling her up. She sucked in her breath as she felt Jack's hands move lower, slipping down to her hips, then to her thighs, as he continued to boost her up, wreaking havoc on her emotions despite her every effort to block everything out except for the rescue. She could feel her face burning as she realized that Jack had a very clear view beneath her skirt. Not a good time to find herself unintentionally going commando.

With a mighty tug, Gloria found herself beside the technician on the floor, whose name was inscribed in white right over his breast pocket. Raul. Offering him a smile of gratitude, she tried to get her bearings as best she could. Regaining her composure was a lost cause.

Jack threw both his jacket and hers over the top, followed by her purse. And in the next moment he was there on the floor beside her, looking a hell of a lot better than she did, she thought ruefully.

"You two all right?" Furrows of concern went all the way up to Raul's pronounced receding hairline as he looked uncertainly from one to the other. "Want me to call the paramedics?"

Jack shook his head. "I'm fine." Sitting up, he looked at Gloria. "How about you?"

Her eyes held his for a long moment. Was he just asking about her condition, or did the question actually go deeper? On the surface, she could answer him with a terse, "Fine." No bones were broken, no health-threatening conditions had to be addressed. Beyond that, she wasn't sure.

All she knew was that everything had been upended and she had no idea if there was a penalty attached to that. A penalty for flying without ever leaving the floor.

Still, if there was, that was her problem, not his.

Taking in another deep, sweet breath of nonrestricted air, she finally nodded. "I'm okay."

The technician was on his feet again, surprisingly agile for a man who appeared at least fifty pounds overweight and beyond his prime by most standards.

"Okay, then." Raul touched each of them on the arm as though discharging them from his care. "I've got other elevators to see to."

As Raul turned to walk away, Jack called after him, "Is all the power back?"

Raul had a one-hundred-watt smile. "Like nothing ever happened, except that the elevators seem to be a little out of sync. But I'll fix that soon enough." He hurried to a stairwell, calling, "Have a nice day" just before he disappeared.

Jack refrained from saying something about the inane statement. Once on his feet, he extended his hand to Gloria and waited. After a beat she locked her fingers around his and rose to stand beside him.

He frowned, concerned about her well-being. "You sure you're all right?"

Aware of how she'd behaved, Gloria tried to laugh

the incident off. "Well, I'm dumping all my stock in this elevator company, but other than being a little bit shaky, yes, I'm all right."

She bit her lip as she looked at him again. Just where did they go from here? Did they talk about what happened in the elevator? Ignore it? Treat it as the first step in a truce or just an aberration they were better off not acknowledging?

She didn't know and she longed for something that she could understand, something familiar she could grasp and hang on to.

Belatedly, she realized that she was still holding his hand. Releasing it, she glanced at his wrist. Where the watch crystal had been were now just a couple of jagged pieces of glass.

"Your watch."

He glanced at it reflexively. "What about it?"

"It's broken." Well, that would explain the sound of breaking glass she'd heard. She'd thought she was just imagining it, along with the swirls of color, heat and music that had gone through her mind just before the elevator had come back to life.

Holding up his wrist, Jack examined it. He shook his head. "So it is."

"I can fix it for you," she volunteered, reaching for it.

Jack pulled back his hand. Right now, the less contact they had, the faster his mind would clear. "No, I—"

A puzzled expression creased her brow before fading away. "It's the least I can do, seeing as how you took my mind off being trapped in the elevator." A sultry smile filtered along her lips.

The comment was enough to temporarily break the tension he was feeling. Jack laughed and took the watch off his wrist, handing it to her. Gloria slipped it into her purse.

"When can I have it back?"

"I'll have it ready for you on your next visit." She raised her eyes to his. "If you'll just tell me when that'll be." Did that sound too much as if she was asking for a date? God, she hoped not.

He hesitated, thinking of his schedule. Thinking, too, that he wanted some time to himself. Because all he could think about right now was making love with her again, which made him feel as uneasy as being faced with a sudden takeover.

"I've got to fly out of town tomorrow." He was due in New York for a quick meeting. Until just now, he'd planned on making a conference call. Now, taking a plane and going back to his home turf sounded like just what the doctor ordered. "How does next Tuesday at ten sound?"

He'd be back before then, but he needed time to get things in perspective.

Gloria pressed her lips together and nodded. Inside, she was banking down a volley of disappointment. She'd hoped that he'd say he would be by tomorrow.

What a difference half an hour made, she thought.

This morning she would have been relieved that he wasn't going to be breathing down her neck. From that vantage point, next Tuesday would have seemed too soon. Now it felt like an eternity.

Get hold of yourself before you fall off the deep end. This isn't the first guy you've ever made love with.

No, but it was the first one who'd caused fireworks to go off in her body and in her head.

Gloria cleared her throat and tried to sound nonchalant. "What are you going to do for a watch until then?"

Back home, he had several different watches, including a Rolex he rarely wore. Most of the time, he favored the one that was now in her possession, but he'd thought to pack another one. He believed in making plans for every contingency.

He just needed to form one for what he was feeling now. "It's not my only watch," he told her.

"Of course not. What was I thinking?"

He couldn't fathom the look on her face. Amused? Rueful? And why did understanding it make such a difference to him?

Damn, but he needed to clear his head.

"It is, however, my favorite. My father gave it to me when I graduated college. It belonged to my grandfather." He couldn't help the grin that curved his mouth. "I bet Grandpa never gave it a workout like that one." Jack nodded toward the elevator.

He liked the way her smile took command of her features, shyly slipping out as if to test the waters, then swiftly blooming over her face. It was like watching the sun rise and take possession of the land.

It certainly took possession of him.

The realization had him backpedaling so quickly, he found himself in danger of getting his foot caught in the spokes. This was happening too fast, throwing him off balance.

It was time to retreat.

Now.

He cleared his throat, looking toward the stairwell the technician had taken. "Well, I was on my way to see my father before all this started," he muttered.

"So you said." She didn't relish taking the stairs with their stale air and their dim lighting. She relished the idea of getting on the elevator far less, no matter what the technician said about the restoration of power. She chose the lesser of two evils and headed toward the stairs.

He was right behind her. She felt safe and threatened at the same time.

She should have remained in the store, she told herself. But she couldn't help the smile that was firmly entrenched on her lips.

Just as he opened the stairwell door and motioned for her to go first, she stopped abruptly. "I, um, think you have something of mine."

He looked at her, a confused expression on his face. She wondered if he knew how adorable he looked.

Probably not the word he would have liked applied to himself, she reasoned, and let the moment go.

"What?" He wanted to know. Was she going to say something lofty, about her heart or something along those lines?

He felt a defensiveness setting in, the kind that was meant to protect men from ever making any kind of commitment beyond which wine they favored with dinner.

Instead of saying anything, she merely looked toward his pocket. It took him a second, then he remembered. Slipping his hand inside, his fingers came into contact with soft lace. As much as he tried to remove himself from the man he'd turned into just a few minutes ago, it wasn't possible. Not when her lacy underwear was rubbing against his skin. Not when he remembered what she'd looked like, her body silhouetted in the auxiliary light, wearing the scrap of material.

"Oh, right." He took them out and looked them over for a second. There was next to nothing to them. Jack grinned. "Wouldn't want you to catch cold, now," he murmured.

She took them from him and stuffed them into her purse. She planned to put them on the moment she could find a ladies' room.

They parted company on the twenty-ninth floor. She went to see Christina, he continued to the next floor to talk to his father.

He could still feel the soft imprint of lace against his palm as he made his way to the thirtieth floor.

* * *

The second she appeared in Christina's office, Gloria found herself enveloped in her sister's embrace.

"Oh, thank God, thank God," Christina cried. "You're okay."

"I'm okay." Gloria's answer was muffled by her sister's shoulder. "Or at least I will be if you let me up for air."

"Oh, I'm sorry." Christina immediately released her. "It's just that I—" She stopped abruptly, taking another look at her sister.

Gloria was holding her coat over her arm. She'd stopped at the ladies' room to reapply her makeup and slip her suit jacket back on, as well as her underwear. She'd felt pretty confident that she'd gotten herself back in order so that there was no evidence of how she and Jack had passed the time while waiting to be rescued.

But beneath Christina's scrutiny, she wasn't nearly as confident as she had been walking out of the ladies' room. She cleared her throat and tried to sound as innocent as possible as she asked, "What?"

"You're glowing," Christina declared. She narrowed her eyes as if to make sure they weren't playing tricks on her. "My God, you're glowing." She shut the door to her office so that no one else could overhear. There was more than a little disbelief as well as curiosity on her face.

"I was half out of my mind when I realized that the power failure hit just as you were probably on your way up. That you were most likely stuck in the elevator. I tried to reach you on your cell and when mine said the signal wasn't getting through, I just *knew* you were in one of the elevators. I felt so guilty and so bad for you."

"Guilty?"

"Because you were coming to see me. But you're glowing," she repeated in awe.

"Well, it was pretty awful," Gloria said. *At least in the beginning.*

Christina circled her slowly, taking in every angle. Her arms were crossed in front of her chest. "Then why aren't you ghostly pale?" she challenged, sounding every bit like an interrogator.

Gloria could feel her cheeks burning. But there was no way she was going to tell Christina what had happened. Not after the way she'd carried on about how they all had to swear off men for their lives to get back on track.

She raised her chin slightly. "I just walked up five fights of stairs. That usually gets people flushed."

Christina read the body language. Despite the years they'd spent apart, she was still familiar with Gloria's moves.

"Flushed, yes," she emphasized pointedly, "but not glowing." She fixed her younger sister with a penetrating look that had edged out the relieved expression she'd been wearing only seconds ago. "Okay, give. What's going on?"

Gloria shifted slightly. Along with gaining sobriety, leaving the shadowy world of alcohol had caused her to lose her ability to lie successfully. She gave it a shot anyway. "Maybe I'm outgrowing my claustrophobia."

Christina eyed her closely. "And maybe there's another explanation."

"Like what?" she asked innocently.

"Like a man. Were you alone in the elevator?"

She was about to say no, but what if Jack told his father that he'd ridden up with her? She knew he wouldn't give Patrick Fortune any explicit details, but still, that would place her in the middle of a lie. She decided to go with the truth, at least partially.

"No, I wasn't."

Like Sherlock Holmes discovering the all-important clue, Christina's face lit up. "Aha."

"No 'aha,' Tina. I was in the elevator with Jack Fortune. You know what I think of him."

Christina was silent for a moment. "Do you remember reading *Macbeth* in college?"

Gloria shook her head. She didn't like the tone of Christina's voice. Or where this conversation was heading. "Nope, sorry, except for my major, college was pretty much a blur."

"There's a line in it about Lady Macbeth. Something about the lady protesting too much."

Gloria pretended that the line—and the insinuation—meant nothing to her. "I guess I'll have to read it sometime."

"Yes," Christina agreed. "You will."

"Let's go to lunch," Gloria urged, wanting to get her sister onto a different topic. "I'm starved."

Christina retrieved her purse out of a drawer. "Okay, let's go catch an elevator."

Just that word brought back all the intimate details of her ride with Jack, and she felt herself blush.

Gloria stared at her watch. It felt as if the minute hand was glued in place, only moving when she looked away. But it was moving. Moving beyond the time that Jack had told her he would be by.

For their meeting. For his watch.

It was Tuesday. Where was he? He was far too controlled to be late, and yet, here he was, late.

Or not coming at all.

She walked around the showroom, annoyance and confusion marking her every step. If he wasn't coming, why hadn't he called?

Turning, she reached for the phone behind the counter, then dropped her hand. It wasn't her place to call him. He'd been the one to arrange the time and the day. He was the one who wasn't here. That meant it was up to him to call, not her.

Frustration nibbled away at her as she continued to roam restlessly.

Gone were the drop cloths, the telltale signs of a shop in transition. The glass displays were all in place, sparkling and ready, their virgin shelves waiting to make first contact with the unique pieces of jewelry she was going to display.

The store was only a few days away from opening. Trying desperately not to dwell on the feelings that had been awakened in that dim elevator car, she'd pushed herself hard to get the shop ready. It had involved calling in favors from previous connections she'd made, pleading with carpet layers, glass cutters, a whole host of people she'd needed to get the place in order. All of her design equipment had been delivered late last night. The safe she'd had put in the day after her elevator encounter now housed the precious gems she had at her disposal.

The security system had cost extra because she'd asked for it to be installed immediately. But the gems were safe. Everything here was state-of-the-art.

She was exhausted, hardly getting five hours of sleep a night, but it was all worth it, every hour, every inconvenience. She was ready.

Gloria looked at her watch again, muttering under her breath. Where was he?

She'd wanted to show Jack everything, to prove to him that she was every bit as savvy a business person as he was. She wanted to impress him, she thought ruefully. Like some young teenage girl showing off for the guy who'd caught her attention. Who'd made her heart race.

Gloria clenched her hands, digging her nails into her palms as she paced, her eyes never far from the glass doors. Waiting for a knock.

Damn it, she was a grown woman, thoughts about impressing men didn't belong in her head.

They weren't in her head, she thought, fighting off mounting despair, they were in her heart and that was the problem.

She'd allowed him to get to her.

What the hell was wrong with her? Didn't she realize where things like that led? Nowhere. Not for her, at least. What did she expect, anyway? Violins? Undying love because they'd made love in an elevator? Even if they had connected, he was only here temporarily. Everything about him told her he was itching to get back home, back to New York.

Home for her was here. She knew that now. They were from two different worlds. Just because she still believed in happy endings didn't mean they were destined to come true. It just meant that she was still harboring illusions.

No, delusions.

She curbed the urge to throw Jack's watch across the showroom, smashing it against the opposite wall. That would be childish and it wouldn't change anything. Even though it probably would make her feel better for a couple of minutes.

Squaring her shoulders, she returned the repaired watch to the box she'd kept it in.

At that very moment Jack was sitting in an office clear across town, frowning at his reflection in the window.

He knew he was supposed to be at the mall, with Gloria, but somehow he couldn't make himself get up out of the chair. Hadn't been able to get up for over an hour now.

Okay, so he was a coward, Jack thought. But even Navy SEALs didn't risk their lives until they knew the lay of the land and what they were getting into. And he had no idea what he was getting into, except that what he had felt in that elevator last week had really scared the hell out of him.

What he'd felt for Gloria Mendoza was too much like the emotion he'd buried along with Ann all those years ago. He didn't want to have those feelings again, didn't want to get involved again.

Besides, the woman was clearly a handful. He liked being in control and he hadn't been, not that day. Not of the situation, not even of himself. It had felt as if all systems were go and he had no idea where it was that they were going. Only that he was hanging on for dear life.

He stared at the phone on the desk. He should at least call, he told himself.

His hand remained still.

He didn't like this side of him. He'd never fled from a fight in his life, but hell, fights he could handle with aplomb, it was the non-fighting part of this that had him stymied.

There was no future in any of this, he insisted silently. The woman drank, just like Ann had. And, just like Ann, she might wind up killing herself. He couldn't live through something like that. Not again.

Besides, he was going back to New York in a couple of weeks. Sooner if he could convince his father that he wasn't needed here any longer.

Why the man had had him come out in the first place was still a mystery. After all, his father had seemed pretty certain of the woman's business acumen. Had sung her praises whenever the opportunity arose.

What the hell did his father need him for?

There were a myriad of questions assaulting him and absolutely no answers.

Chapter Thirteen

Gloria was across the room when the phone in the showroom finally rang.

For the past hour she'd been attempting to convince herself that she didn't care one way or another if Jack called. She'd pretended to be distracted with setting up several pieces of new equipment in the back office. But the second the phone rang, she'd raced to answer it, all the while wondering why he hadn't tried to contact her on her cell. Was the battery running low?

"Hello?" She covered the mouthpiece so Jack couldn't hear her breathing hard.

His deep voice resonated in her ear. "I'm not going to make the appointment."

There wasn't a single note of apology in the statement, nothing. Gloria's back went up. She felt like an idiot, watching the clock and waiting for him. *Once an idiot, always an idiot,* a small voice taunted her.

"I kind of figured that out on my own, seeing as how you said ten and it's after twelve now."

"There's a lot of traffic on the road."

Didn't she even merit something a little more inventive than that excuse?

"I suppose there would have to be, considering that there are several ways to get here." She reined in her temper, but it wasn't easy. Did he think she was a fool? "How long do you think the traffic is going to continue?" she asked sarcastically.

There was a pause on the other end, as if he was thinking over her question. Or fabricating an answer. "Can't really say. Why don't we just cancel?"

She felt something freeze in her heart. "Today or forever?"

"What?"

She couldn't tell whether he hadn't heard her or was annoyed with her question. Either way, she didn't feel like repeating herself. "Never mind." She stared at the box in front of her on the counter. "I've fixed your watch," she reminded him.

"Fine." He sounded distracted, as if this was difficult for him. Did he have trouble lying to her because he cared or because he lacked creativity? "I'll get back to you on that."

"Fine," she echoed.

But it wasn't. It wasn't fine at all. It was incredibly painful.

He'd hung up and she found herself listening to a dial tone.

Wanting to strangle him.

The man was running, she thought. Running for his life.

She dropped the receiver into the cradle. Boy, she could sure pick 'em, couldn't she? Gloria shoved the watch away from her before she was tempted to drop it on the floor.

When was she going to learn? She'd allowed herself to climb out on that limb again, the one that left her vulnerable and exposed, and for what? For a man who was obviously scared out of his mind by the idea of commitment. She wouldn't have thought that of him, but there it was, he was trying to pull off a vanishing act.

"Okay," she murmured to the telephone. "I'm going to make this really easy for you, Jack."

Picking up the receiver, she began to dial another number.

Patrick Fortune thoughtfully regarded the young woman walking into his office that Tuesday afternoon. She looked pale, but other than that, even more exceptional than the last time he had seen her. There was a fire in her eyes that had been missing then. He wondered if it had to do with his son. He certainly hoped so.

"I'll call you back, dear," he told his wife. "Yes, I love you, too."

Hearing him, Gloria found herself wishing that Jack had taken after his father in the most important things.

Patrick gestured to the antique chair in front of his desk. "Take a seat," he invited, then peered more closely at her. "You look a little pale, Gloria, would you like some water?"

"No, thank you. It was just the ride up in the elevator," she explained.

Although, if she were being honest, she'd have to admit that she'd been feeling out of sync before she'd even set foot in it. She blamed it on Jack. He'd thrown her entire system off ever since the elevator incident.

With the carelessness of a man who was accustomed to being the center of female attention, he'd wantonly yanked her into a space where she was utterly vulnerable, dreaming dreams that would never come true.

Patrick filled in what he felt she'd left unsaid. "Afraid of another blackout? I assure you that it's not going to happen again. I've seen to it that we have a new, state-of-the-art generator as backup, the kind they use in hospitals." He studied her expression for a moment. "But you don't really care about that, do you, Gloria?"

"No, sir." She took the box that contained Jack's watch out of her purse and placed it on the desk. She saw Patrick eyeing it, though he made no attempt to reach for the box. "I was wondering if you could do me two favors. First, would you please give this to Jack?" She pushed the box farther toward him.

Patrick raised a brow and Gloria nodded, silently permitting him to open the box. A quizzical expression came over his face. "This is his grandfather's watch." He knew how much the watch meant to his son. Had Jack given it to her as some kind of token of his affection? Was she breaking it off between them now for some reason?

"I know," she acknowledged. "He told me. I replaced the crystal for him. It broke," she tagged on, hoping Jack's father wouldn't think to ask how his son had come to break it.

It was obvious that he still didn't understand why she was asking him to act as a go-between. "Why don't you give it to him yourself?"

Okay, here we go. "That's the second favor. I appreciate everything you've done for me, I really do, but if you don't mind, I'd rather go it alone from here on in. Meaning, without Jack," she added in case he thought she was turning down his generous loan, as well. "I have enough business experience—"

"No one's doubting that, Gloria. I just wanted to take some of the burden off your shoulders."

She sat up a little straighter. "My shoulders are fine, sir. They're stronger than they look."

A smile curved his thin lips. "Yes, I know." When she looked at him, a confused expression on her beautiful face, he explained, "Your mother's been filling me in a little about what you've gone through. And how you fought your way back. It couldn't have been easy." He looked genuinely impressed. "You're to be commended."

Gloria looked down at her hands. "Thank you," she murmured, embarrassed. And then she realized that Patrick had given her the perfect way out. "So you understand, I want to do this my way."

He understood more than she thought. Patrick shook his head. "Been giving you trouble, has he?"

She began to protest, then thought there was no sense in it. The man could probably see right through her. "Yes."

Patrick laughed softly to himself. "He's very stubborn. I'm afraid he gets that from me."

The difference was, when Jack's father was being stubborn, he made you think it was your idea and not his that he was sponsoring. A rueful smile slid across her lips. "Someone forgot to give him your charm."

The compliment brought a smile to his eyes.

Patrick could already envision the young jeweler as his daughter-in-law. The more he saw her, the more he learned about her, the more convinced he was that Gloria was just the kind of woman Jack needed in his life. His equal, an independent woman who could stand on her own two feet and yet could complete a union by her very presence. In a way, she reminded him a little of his own wife, Lacey. Jack could do a lot worse.

His smile was warm as he regarded her. He'd been

flattered by the best. But in this case, she sounded sincere. "Exercising a little of your own charm right now, aren't you?"

"I wouldn't know about that, I just—" She stopped abruptly as she saw Patrick Fortune raise his eyes to look at someone behind her. Shifting in her seat, for a split second she felt just the slightest bit dizzy. What she saw didn't help any. Her eyes narrowed. "Traffic clear up for you?"

"'Traffic'?" Patrick echoed, looking from one to the other for an explanation. The expressway beyond his window was moving rapidly without a mishap in sight.

"Yes." She never took her eyes off Jack. "He missed our appointment this morning because he said there was too much traffic."

Now things were starting to make sense, Patrick thought. Right now, he was standing hip-deep in the middle of a lovers' quarrel and if he didn't leave quickly, he might be hit in the crossfire.

Rising, he addressed his son although he was nodding at Gloria. "Gloria came to me, asking that you be removed as adviser." He wasn't about to cite her reasons. "I'll let the two of you sort this out."

Removed as adviser. It was exactly what he wanted, exactly what he'd come by to propose—again—to his father. But the fact that she had asked for it stung, wounding his male pride.

He felt as if he'd just been pushed away. Rejected. It wasn't a pretty feeling.

"There's no need for you to leave—" Jack began to protest, only to have his father wave a hand at him. He didn't notice the uneasiness on Gloria's face.

Patrick gave his son a meaningful look. "Oh, but I think there is. I think there's plenty of need." And then he smiled again. "Until later, Gloria." With that, Patrick began to take his leave. As he walked past his son, he paused to say, "Oh, by the way, she wanted me to give you this." He thrust the dark-blue box into his son's hand and walked out of the office.

Gloria couldn't take her eyes off Jack. Pinpricks of anticipation ran along her body, jabbing at her. Jack was staring down at the box in his hand. And then, as he flipped it open to examine the contents, she saw anger crease his brow.

He looked up at her. "You didn't have to come here to leave this."

She was still feeling as though someone had borrowed her personality and left ashes in its wake. Hurt warred with anger and she let go of the temper she normally kept curbed.

"Why shouldn't I come here to drop it off? You certainly weren't going to stop by to pick it up anytime soon. You were stuck in 'traffic.' Just where was this mythical traffic, Jack? I got here without encountering any. I guess they must all have been following you around because they certainly weren't out on the road when I got on it."

Annoyed over being caught in the halfhearted lie

he'd given her, Jack made an attempt at an explanation. "Gloria—"

But Gloria was on her feet, her hands raised in front of her, ready to bat away anything he said.

"No. I get it. I do," she insisted. "You're uncomfortable over what happened in the elevator." Once she started, the words she'd been harboring in her heart just poured out. "I don't know if you're just ashamed of letting your guard down, or ashamed because you'd let it down with me—"

"Gloria—"

"But it doesn't matter. The end result is that you're ashamed, or unnerved, or whatever you want to call it. Bottom line, being around me makes you uncomfortable. Well, you don't have to be around me any longer. I just took care of that for you."

"I am not ashamed," he finally managed to snap at her.

That gave her absolutely no solace. "But you are uncomfortable."

He thought of lying, but she would probably know he was. "Yes."

That hurt more than she'd expected, even though she'd been the one to say it first. "Fine, so we understand each other—" Turning on her heel, her stomach churning and her head pounding, she headed for the door.

Jack knew he should just let her go. In the long run, that would be easier and they'd both get a little peace.

But something inside him wouldn't allow it. He didn't want her going, not like this. Not without some kind of an explanation. It was important that she understand why he was uncomfortable.

The thought almost made him laugh. Hell, how could she understand any of this when he was having trouble understanding it all himself?

But even so, he moved swiftly, catching up to her at the door. His arm went out across the opening, barring her way. "No, we don't. We don't understand each other—"

She gritted her teeth together. It occurred to him that he had never seen a woman look as magnificent as she did at this moment.

"Get out of my way." When he made no move to lower his arm, she told him, "I warn you, my brother taught me a lot of self-defense moves."

"Good for him." Jack took a deep breath. If he didn't say it now, he never would. "I was engaged once."

"What?" The idea was utterly foreign to her. She just couldn't picture him making any kind of an emotional commitment.

Couldn't she?

When she'd made love with him, she'd made love with the man she'd discovered beneath the gruff exterior, the man who didn't ridicule her fears, but held her and tried to make her feel safe. And she had. For a short time, she had felt safe.

Something told her she wasn't going to want to hear

what he had to tell her. Still, she couldn't make herself push her way out. She had to hear what he was going to say. "Go on."

Each word felt as if he was pulling it out of some deep abyss. "It was while I was in college. Her name was Ann Garrison and I loved her."

Jealousy flashed through her like a pan fire. She clamped down a lid on it. "A lot?"

Why was she torturing herself like this?

Maybe it was because she needed him to say this to help her walk away, to make herself realize once and for all that there was no future with him.

"A lot," he echoed. She watched his eyes soften as he spoke of the woman he'd wanted to share his name. "She had this zest for life, this way of plunging into things." He looked at her. "A lot like you."

The comparison both warmed her and chilled her heart. He'd loved someone. And it wasn't her. Wouldn't be her. "What happened?"

"Along with her zest, she liked to party." He paused, looking for the right words. He didn't find them. The words that emerged from his mouth were blunt. And so was the pain. "And drink. She said that drinking just made her feel even happier." The shrug that accompanied the words was helpless. "I was young, I figured she could handle it. I did." Although, looking back, he'd consumed a great deal less than Ann had. "She, um, wanted to go for a ride one evening after having more than her share of margaritas at a local restaurant."

Each word was painful, filled with thorns that ripped at his throat as he uttered them. "At first, I told her no. I even tried to take the keys away from her, but she insisted she was fine and that I was worrying too much. I did worry when it came to her," he admitted. He should have stuck to his guns instead of indulging her. That was always his mistake, indulging her. "So I went with her, thinking that my being there would somehow protect her."

How stupid could he have been? Jack upbraided himself. But when you were twenty-two, you thought you were immortal. He learned differently.

He took a deep breath, then released it. "It didn't. It didn't protect her, or the driver in the truck she hit." His voice quavered. "I doubt if she even saw it coming." He remembered shouting a warning, but it had been too late. "She slammed into the truck head-on. I was knocked out." As he spoke he relived the moment. Jack felt as if someone was sitting on his chest.

"When I came to, the paramedics were putting her in a body bag. They put me in an ambulance. I was too hurt to stand up. I couldn't get to her, couldn't hold her one last time." His voice threatened to crack and he paused, trying to gather himself together. He looked at Gloria. Were those tears in her eyes? He couldn't tell. "Something died inside of me with Ann that night." This was what he wanted her to understand. What couldn't happen between them wasn't her fault, it was his. "I can't feel anything."

He was lying to her, she thought. She heard what he wasn't saying. That the woman he loved had had a drinking problem. Just like her. Having her tell him that she'd had one, too, had brought back all his fears. In his own way, he probably hated her for stirring them all up again. For making him think of Ann.

"I see."

Her words were almost inaudible. And strained. "I'm not sure you do," Jack countered. He tried again. "I want to care about you, but—"

"You're afraid I'm going to get drunk and plow my car into someone." She forced herself to freeze the anger she felt, afraid that it might spill out, red-hot, burning them both.

"No," he protested.

She shook her head, stopping him from continuing. "I could always spot a liar, Jack. Maybe because I told so many lies myself while I was bingeing. Lies to spare other people. Lies to spare myself. In the end, they all come back to haunt you."

She looked at Jack, wishing he could see inside of her. Wishing she could make him believe what she was saying.

"I've been sober for two years now and I have it under control. Cured? No. Tempted? Yes. When I'm stressed, upset, the craving comes back, whispering that if I just have this one drink, everything's going to be all right, going to be rosy. But I know it's not. And if I have that one drink, I know that I'm going to have to start all over again. I'm going to have to start counting again from day one. That's too hard, too demeaning." A small, sad smile curved her lips. "I'm a very competitive person, Jack. Ask anyone in my family. I don't like starting all over again."

He caught her in a lie. It didn't make him happy. "But you relocated your shop—"

Gloria shook her head. Was he trying to trip her up? The thought stung.

"Not the same thing. Relocating doesn't mean starting from scratch. I've got my clientele via the Internet and all those customers out in Hollywood. They'd do business with me if I relocated to the moon."

She knew they had no future, but she wanted him to understand this much about her. About the woman his father was backing.

"I'm not going to drink again because I didn't like myself then. I was weak, unable to handle things. Unable to stand up without a crutch. That wasn't really standing, it was leaning." Her eyes held his. "I like myself sober a lot better."

She believed what she was saying, he thought. He wanted to believe her, as well. But he couldn't. Couldn't risk being burned again. "Still, you could slip—"

"And tomorrow might never come," she countered. "We live in dangerous times, Jack. Everything we see around us might be gone in a matter of hours, you never know. It's up to us to take our happiness where we find it." She wasn't getting through, she realized. The armor plating around his heart was too thick. She had to stop beating her head against it.

"I'm sorry you lost Ann, really sorry you went through all that, but I'm not about to spend each day trying to convince you that I'm not Ann. That's not a battle I'm ready to take on."

His face hardened. "I'm not asking you to."

"Good, then we understand each other—finally," she added. She looked at the arm that was still barring her way. "Now, are you going to lower your arm or do I have to crouch to get under it?"

He said nothing for a moment that stretched out so long she thought it was going to snap like a thin thread. In her heart, she kept hoping that Jack would pick a third alternative to the ones she'd given him. That he'd tell her she was right, that he was wrong and that he wanted to try again. That she meant enough to him for him to *want* to try again.

When he dropped his arm, allowing her to leave, she thought her heart was going to drop into her stomach. She could feel it tying itself up into a huge, unmanageable knot.

With her head held high, she walked out. Biting her lip to keep the tears back.

Chapter Fourteen

Gloria had been carrying around the small, innocuous-looking box in her purse for almost a week now, unable to open it and put it to use. Unable to face what might be the possible results.

But it was time to face things now.

Yesterday had marked the grand opening of her store and Jack hadn't come by. Not at all. He hadn't even bothered to call. Oh, he'd sent her flowers, big, beautiful pink roses; two dozen in an overwhelming arrangement. They'd been accompanied by a generic note that read "Good luck" and could have been sent to his shoemaker with the same amount of warmth it generated.

A single flower with a handwritten note would have meant infinitely more.

Everyone else she knew had stopped by. Her parents, her sisters and brother, old friends, even Patrick Fortune—and she knew his schedule was packed to the limit.

So when Jack didn't even bother to pick up the phone to call her with some lame excuse as to why he couldn't make it, she knew she had to face the fact that whatever was between them was over before it had ever had a chance to really take root.

Except, perhaps, for one thing.

She'd had unsettled stomachs before, for a whole myriad of reasons, but this…this felt different. This didn't feel like nerves the way she was desperately trying to convince herself it was. This felt strange. And mornings were the worst.

And none worse than this morning.

Her parents had insisted on having the five of them, her brother, sisters and her, over to dinner to celebrate the store's grand opening. At first she'd begged off, wanting to be alone with her hurt. But her mother had insisted and, eventually, Gloria had decided that maybe it was better to have people she loved around her. She'd hoped that they would take her mind off the pain of being ignored by the one man she'd thought would make a difference in her life.

The man she realized she was in love with, no good rotten so-and-so that he was.

Maria Mendoza had seemed so thrilled to have almost all of her children under one roof again that when she suggested they all remain for the night, no one had the heart to turn her down. After all, it was only for the one night.

But alone in her old room, Gloria found that her thoughts wouldn't leave her alone. Her thoughts and her unhappy stomach.

Morning found her throwing up.

She had to face the music. So she dug out the box that had all but become a permanent companion and set it on the bathroom counter. She stared at it for close to ten minutes before she finally opened the box and followed the directions she had already committed to memory.

Waiting was agony.

Discovery was worse.

The stick was blue. She was pregnant.

Pregnant with the baby of a man who was going to be flying out of her life any day now. She strained her eyes, hoping to see the color fade into pink. But it didn't.

Her knees buckled beneath her and she sank down onto the closed commode, feeling numb all over, a numbness that was climbing up into her throat, threatening to gag her.

Damn it, what had she been thinking to allow this to happen?

She hadn't been thinking, that was the problem. Instead of being logical, she'd been feeling. For the first time in a long, long time, she'd let her feelings loose and it had been wonderful.

Looking back, she had to admit that the wild rush of being in love had been nothing short of exhilarating. But she had to squelch it now. That part of the wild ride was over. She had to think about what was ahead. And the baby she was going to have.

She covered her face with one hand. Oh, God, she couldn't deal with this. Her hormones in flux, she felt absolutely lost and alone. The sensation threatened to swallow her up whole.

Still holding the stick as disbelief ricocheted through her, Gloria began to sob. Huge, racking sobs that shook her whole body.

She wasn't exactly sure when she realized she wasn't alone. Looking up, she saw that Sierra was standing in the doorway. Her younger sister looked confused.

Gloria realized that Sierra was looking at the stick she was still clutching in her hand as if it was a wand that had malfunctioned. Belatedly, she tossed it into the wastepaper basket. It fell into the box that had previously housed it.

Coming to life, Sierra quickly closed the door behind her, locked it and knelt beside her sister. "Gloria, what's wrong?"

Gloria pressed her lips together. A sprinkling of the loneliness ebbed away for a second. She tried to smile, but couldn't. "It's just like me to forget to lock the door."

Sierra clearly wasn't about to be diverted by any flip remarks. She honed in on the source of her sister's distress. "The stick was blue."

"Yes," Gloria acknowledged quietly, "the stick was blue." The words, as she said them, felt like a death sentence.

Sierra's shapely brows pulled together in abject confusion. "How can the stick be blue if you're not dating anyone?" And then her eyes opened wide. "You broke the pact."

"No, I didn't. Not exactly. Technically, I'm not dating anyone." She was clutching at straws, trying to save face. Looking for excuses she knew were less than flimsy.

Sierra looked down at the light-blue wastebasket, nodding at the box. "Then this is what, the Angel Gabriel making another middle-of-the-night visit, this time to your old room?"

Gloria dragged a hand through her hair, at a loss as to how to explain. "It happened in the elevator."

Sierra stared at her, struggling to find a plausible explanation. This wasn't it. "The Angel Gabriel appeared to you in an elevator?"

"No," Gloria snapped, then looked at Sierra contritely. Emotions storm-trooped through her, making her want to laugh and cry at the same time. "It was Jack Fortune."

This made almost as little sense. "*He* appeared in the elevator?"

She shook her head. She'd told her sister about the blackout, leaving out a few salient details. "No, he was in the elevator with me when the power went out."

Sierra frowned. "Obviously not all the power." Her sister paused and then her jaw dropped open. "Did he force himself on you?"

If anything, the man had tried to restrain himself, she thought. "It was more like mutual spontaneous combustion." She tried to compose herself.

Sierra asked the million-dollar question. "Does he know?"

Gloria rolled her eyes. "*I* didn't even know until this morning."

"So what are you going to do?" This was her big sister, the one she'd always admired even when she'd sided with Christina. Gloria always had all the answers, even if some of them had been wrong. But this was an entirely new ball field they found themselves playing on.

"I don't know." Gloria stifled another sob, not wanting to cry in front of her sister. Her shoulders shook from the effort and she pretended to shrug them. "Have the baby." That much she was sure of. It was the steps afterward that were so uncertain.

"And?" Sierra prodded.

Gloria tried to think, to channel the new person she had become, that of a confident businesswoman. It wasn't easy. Right now she felt like a lost child who just wanted someone to take care of her.

Finally she said, "And try to pick up the pieces of my life again." She forced a halfhearted smile to her lips. "I'm getting really good at picking up the pieces."

Rising, Sierra placed her hand on Gloria's shoulder. "Aren't you going to tell Jack?"

She wanted to. But she knew she couldn't. At least, not yet. "I don't think Jack really wants to have anything to do with me."

Shock, followed by anger, leaped into her sister's eyes. "What? The rotten bastard gets you pregnant and then bows out?"

"He's *not* a rotten bastard," Gloria cried defensively, her emotions escalating again. She could call him that, but no one else could. It took her a second to get herself under control again. "It's a long story, Sierra. And I already told you, he doesn't know I'm pregnant." She saw the look in her sister's eyes. "And he's not going to know, understand?" Gloria warned. "Not until I'm ready to say something to him. Right now, I couldn't deal with an offer of marriage out of pity and I *really* couldn't deal with him not making the offer." She knew that didn't make any sense to anyone but her. She was between a rock and a hard place.

Gloria rose and grabbed her sister by the shoulders. "Please, Sierra, promise me you won't say anything."

Sierra set her jaw stubbornly. "He has a right to know so he can do the right thing."

"Oh, God, no," Gloria groaned. The last thing she

wanted was for him to "do the right thing." She wanted him to do it because he loved her, not because it was right. She felt weary, anxious and angry at the same time. "The way I feel right now, he *has* no rights. Besides, he's going back to New York."

"Gloria…"

She shut her eyes to the pleading look on her sister's face. She was *not* going to tell Jack anything, not until she was calmer. "I will handle this in my own way."

No you won't, Maria Mendoza thought as she stood on the other side of the door, listening. She'd been drawn by the sobs she'd heard, her mother's heart alerting her that one of her children was hurting.

Gloria had been subdued all last evening. The most gregarious of her brood, her daughter had attempted to put on a happy face, but Maria could see that there was something wrong. It was right there, in her daughter's eyes. She'd slipped out of bed this morning to talk to her privately.

But Gloria's room had been empty. Except for the sobs. She was just about to walk into the bathroom from the opposite entrance when she'd heard Sierra enter from the hall. Something had made her stay where she was. Maria had been rewarded for her restraint with Gloria's story.

It was obvious that her daughter was in love with Jack. The only one who probably didn't realize it was Gloria. And possibly Jack.

She was going to fix that.

* * *

"You are going to throw another party," Maria announced to her husband as she walked back into their bedroom.

Jose was still in bed, trying to steal a few extra minutes before he had to get up to go to the restaurant. They opened at noon, but there was a great deal to do every morning before then.

Accustomed to his wife's ways after all these years, Jose smiled indulgently. "And just when did I decide this?"

Maria glanced over her shoulder. The bathroom door remained closed. Sierra was still in there with Gloria. She shut her own bedroom door. "A few minutes ago."

"I see. Any particular reason I'm throwing this party?"

Maria came around to Jose's side and sat on the edge of the bed. "To celebrate your daughter's grand opening, of course."

"Of course." He pretended to look befuddled. "Wasn't that what last night was about?"

Maria waved her hand, her mind already racing with plans and ideas. The first of which involved calling Patrick Fortune and asking for his help. "That was just for the family. This will be bigger."

"I never doubted it for a moment."

Jose looked at his wife. His feelings hadn't changed about her since the first moment he'd laid eyes on her. She was still the most beautiful woman in the world. Hooking his arm around her waist, he pulled her to him. Maria squealed in protest, but not too loudly.

He paused only long enough to nuzzle her neck. "I will leave it all up to you, as always. Just tell me what you need."

Maria kissed him with all the love that she felt. "You are a good man, Jose."

"Yes, I know. And now the good man must get up and go to work. Call me at the restaurant." Throwing back the covers, he swung his legs over the side of the bed. "By the way, when is this party going to be?"

"Tomorrow."

"Call me quickly," he advised as he went off to take a shower.

Patrick had trouble containing his smile. He felt as if it would come bursting out at any moment. But for now, he needed to keep it all under wraps. Otherwise his firstborn would know something was up.

He looked at Jack now. The latter looked restless, as if he wanted to be somewhere else. Back in New York, perhaps? Away from the source of his delightful dilemma? Patrick bit back that question, as well.

Finally, Jack was the one who broke the silence. "You said you had something to ask me?" he prodded.

"Yes. I'd like you to postpone leaving for a couple of days, Jack."

Jack had been afraid of that. But all things being equal, he wanted to get back to his home ground. And as fast as possible. Maybe then he'd get a decent night's sleep. A night in which he wouldn't have visions of a black-haired she-devil who made him want to throw caution to the wind.

He was too old for that, he insisted silently. Too old to buy into never-ending happiness. "My reservation's already made."

The answer didn't appear to faze his father. "Reservations can be changed."

A flash of temper came and went, taking him by surprise. He'd never been truly annoyed with his father, not even during his teen years when those kinds of reactions were supposed to be commonplace.

"You still need me here?"

"In a matter of speaking." He kept the thought that he wanted Jack to oversee the San Antonio office to himself for the time being. He could spring that on him later. For now, he needed to get Jack to agree to tonight. "I didn't really bring you here to oversee Gloria's new business." He saw Jack eyeing him warily. "I asked you to fly out because I'm worried about you."

"Worried?" Jack mouthed the word as though it were foreign.

"Yes, worried." Patrick came around from behind his desk and placed a paternal arm around his son's shoulders. "You don't seem to ever have any fun, Jack."

His father's words immediately brought an image of Gloria to mind. Gloria, her shapely body sleek with perspiration as they made love in the elevator. He quickly banked down the thought before it took over his body. "I don't need any fun."

"Trust me, you do."

Pausing, Patrick looked at his firstborn intently. Jack had never given him one moment's concern. Until now. He knew how much his son had suffered when Ann had been killed. But that was years ago. It was time to resurrect his heart.

"We live in the moment, Jack. The past is gone, we plan for the future, but we *live* in the moment," he insisted. Then he looked at his son pointedly. "We can't relive the past, and we can't change it no matter how much we want to." He searched Jack's face to see if he was getting through, but his son's expression was a mask. Patrick pressed on. "All we have is the moment, to form our futures as well as our pasts. Don't let your moments slip away, Jack. Don't become married to the bank. It's a very cold, demanding mistress. It can't give you a family."

"It can give me little branch offices." And then he laughed, shaking his head. "I didn't think I'd still be getting advice from my father at forty."

Patrick smiled. "You're never too old to be smart, Jack." He tabled the lecture, knowing if he pushed too hard, he'd just succeed in pushing Jack away from doing what was best for him. "Now then, Maria and Jose Mendoza are throwing a party tonight to celebrate the opening of Gloria's store."

That was what he was afraid of. It had taken a great deal of effort on his part to avoid going to the shop Friday. He'd won that battle, he wasn't about to race onto another battlefield. "I can't—"

"You can and you will." Jack raised an eyebrow. His father's tone brooked no argument. The last time he'd used that tone with him, Jack was eight years old and had decided to march off to Central Park before his father had had a chance to curtail his journey. "You handled the details of setting her up."

Now there his father was wrong. "She handled her own details and I just rubber-stamped everything. In case you hadn't noticed, she's a very headstrong, independent woman."

Patrick didn't bother to hide his smile. "Yes, I noticed." And their children would be just as maddeningly stubborn. He couldn't wait to meet them. "Like the rest of her family. These are very proud people, Jack. You can't insult them by not showing up. At least for a little while."

There was suspicion in his son's eyes. "How little a while?"

Patrick's answer was innocence personified. "An hour. Two at the most. Do it for me."

Jack sighed. He couldn't turn his father down without arousing the older man's suspicions and the last thing he wanted to do was to talk about the feelings that Gloria had aroused within him. Or that he was desperately trying to resist sweeping the woman into his arms and telling her that he loved her.

He *couldn't* love her. Because he just didn't want to leave himself open to heartache again.

Jack sighed. "All right. I'll go. But only for an hour."

Triumph underscored Patrick's smile. "That's all I ask."

An hour, Patrick thought, should be enough time to turn this situation around. Maria had called him yesterday morning. He'd discovered over his first cup of coffee that he was about to be a grandfather. The rest of the details had quickly followed, including the one about his grandchild's mother not telling his son that they were about to become parents.

The thought brought a flutter to his heart every time he thought about it. When he'd called his wife to tell her, Lacey had been over the moon about the latest addition to the Fortune family.

And so would Jack, once he knew. Because, damn it, the man was in love with that woman, even if he refused to admit it to himself. For the past week he'd watched Jack restlessly push his way from one day to the next, a man wrestling with some personal demon he wasn't about to share.

Each time he'd asked him, Jack had said he hadn't been to see Gloria. And each time he'd responded, his son had seemed more restless.

Young people, he'd thought with a shake of his head. They wasted so much time being stubborn.

When Maria had told him about the baby, he'd tried to envision a perfect combination of his son and Gloria. Jack was driven, intelligent and darkly good-looking. Gloria was smart as a whip, gregarious and one of the most beautiful women he had ever seen. Their babies were going to be awe-inspiring.

He wasn't about to let his son make the biggest mistake of his life by walking away from this woman without at least trying to resolve things. And, bless Maria, she even had a plan how to get the two of them together. Simple, but perfect.

"The party is at seven-thirty tonight," he told Jack. "We can go together in the limo."

Jack was already thinking of how to make his escape. He wasn't about to have his father talk him into staying longer. With any luck, he could avoid Gloria altogether. There would probably be a crowd around her, vying for her attention.

"If you don't mind, Dad, I'll drive myself over. That way you can stay as long as you like and I can leave after that hour I promised you." He looked at his father pointedly.

Patrick's smile was indulgent, but he was not about to be put off. "That's all right. Simon can come back and get me after he takes you home." As Jack opened his mouth to protest, his father overrode him. "I pay him an obscenely high salary to do things like that."

Having no choice, Jack was forced to agree.

Patrick sensed his son's displeasure as the younger man left the office. He smiled to himself as he reached for the telephone.

The woman picked up on the first ring.

"He's coming," was all he said. Warm laughter filled his ear.

"You are an angel, Patrick," Maria declared.

"No, just a hopeful grandfather," Patrick contradicted. And then he hung up, wanting to call Lacey again to tease her about being a grandmother.

Chapter Fifteen

"I want you to think about relocating here. Permanently."

His father's words echoed within the limousine, taking Jack completely by surprise. A moment ago he'd been looking out at the darkened landscape as they drove to the Mendoza home just outside of Red Rock, thinking how much he missed the never-ending activity of New York. He definitely hadn't seen this coming.

Jack shifted in his seat, looking at his father. For the first time it occurred to him that perhaps the man he had looked up to and respected all of his life really didn't know him. How could he, if he'd just made him this offer?

"Dad, I really appreciate the offer but—"

Patrick raised his hand, forestalling the words that were coming. "Just think about it," his father requested. "You don't have to give me an answer right away."

Jack saw no point in delaying the inevitable. "You know what my answer's going to be whether I give it to you now or later."

The smile on Patrick's lips was enigmatic. "Nothing is ever a sure thing, son."

He didn't want to seem ungrateful or to buck some master plan his father had conceived, but the sooner he got out of San Antonio, the better. He missed New York, but far more important, he needed to put some space between himself and Gloria. She was what he missed most of all and being so close was playing havoc on his willpower.

"You don't need me, Dad. You just transferred Derek here."

But Patrick wouldn't retract the offer. In his quiet, forceful way, he was adamant. "And he's your best friend. You're the one who brought him to me in the first place, remember? You two work well together."

His few encounters with Derek out here had left him feeling very competitive with his friend. It had made him take a step back to reassess the situation.

He decided that honesty was the best way to go, at least about work. "Yes, we do, but I thought you were grooming him to take over operations."

Patrick was silent for a moment, as if weighing his

words carefully. Jack wondered if it was because his father was trying not to hurt him. "The bank's gotten too big to hand off to just one man, Jack. And if it weren't too big, I would have handed it over to you. You're the one I've been grooming all these years." A smile quirked his lips before it ruefully faded. "Maybe overgrooming. You need some fun in your life."

Jack sighed and shook his head. "So you keep telling me."

Patrick straightened in his seat as the limousine pulled into the Mendoza driveway. Jack noticed that his father looked oddly alert, the way he always did when he was on the verge of an important merger.

"All right, we're here," Patrick said, rubbing his hands together in anticipation. "No more talk about work for the duration of the evening, all right?"

Jack thought it pointless to remind his father that he was only staying for an hour. Less, if he could arrange it. "Whatever you say."

The passenger door opened. The chauffeur stepped back, allowing them to get out. Patrick flashed a smile over his shoulder at his son as he disembarked. "That's what I like to hear."

She didn't want to be at a party, much less a party being thrown in her honor. But there just didn't seem to be any way to say no to her mother. For some reason, the woman seemed very excited about the idea of this party. Besides, Gloria thought, she'd said no to the woman far too often while she'd been a teenager and then in her early twenties. If having her here, rubbing her elbows with well-wishers, made her mother happy, Gloria supposed it was the least she could do.

And if she had to constantly force a smile to her face as one person and then another tried to get her attention, well, at least it kept her mind off her problems.

Off the baby that was growing inside of her.

Clutching a glass of ginger ale, she took a sip and nodded at something that a friend of her brother's was saying to her. Her mind was miles away.

How in heaven's name was she going to tell her parents that she was going to have a baby?

She knew they were hugely supportive and that she could rely on them for absolutely anything, but she also knew that this was going to hurt them. Times might have changed, but pride hadn't. Bringing a child into the family without having a husband in tow was still going to be an embarrassment for them, no matter what they said to the contrary.

But they would deal with it, because they loved her. She was secure in that love, but she still didn't look forward to that initial moment when she saw them trying to hide their surprise and disappointment.

As if materializing out of her thoughts, her mother came up behind her. The slender fingers that had knitted and sewn countless things for her over the years took hold of her shoulders.

Her mother's hands felt unusually icy. Gloria shivered.

"Oh, you feel so warm," Maria declared with a touch of envy in her voice and then she sighed. "My blood doesn't seem to want to move through this tired old body very much."

Gloria turned around to face her mother. Maria Mendoza was not anyone's idea of "old." Just what was she up to? Gloria wondered.

"That's because the rest of you is flying around. Maybe your blood is just sitting back, preparing for the next explosion." Then, because she did look somewhat chilled despite the warmth in the room, Gloria handed her glass to her mother and began to strip her shawl from her shoulders. "Here, you want my shawl?"

Maria stayed her hand immediately, shaking her dark head. "No, it looks so pretty on you, *querida*. Leave it on."

"I don't mind," Gloria insisted. "If you're cold—"

Maria gave her what Gloria always thought of as her "mothering" look. "You can be a dear and go get mine for me." Her mother slipped her arm through hers, gently tugging her toward the stairs. "It's in my bedroom. In the bureau. Bottom drawer. On the left." Each additional instruction was given as she pushed her daughter off in the right direction.

At the bottom of the stairs, Gloria nodded. At least it would give her a little respite from the crowd, she thought. She grasped the spiral, light-maple wood banister. "Sure, be right back."

Maria smiled to herself as she watched Gloria go up the stairs.

* * *

Jack roamed around the master bedroom, feeling restless. The king-size four-poster that dominated the room was laden with coats and jackets. The scent of old wood and fresh polish subtly wafted through the air, mingling lightly with the cologne that Maria Mendoza favored.

It seemed like a strange place for a meeting.

A strange place for a man who had been acting strangely.

Jack shoved his hands into his pockets. There were no two ways about it, his father had been acting very strangely of late. They'd had all that time to talk in the limousine as they were coming up here and instead the man had asked him to meet with him in the Mendoza's master bedroom.

Rolling it over in his mind now, it sounded a little clandestine to Jack, especially since his father had said earlier that they were tabling all talk about business while they were at the party.

But the fact that he did want to talk about work heartened Jack. Maybe his father was coming back to his senses. Maybe there was something about work that couldn't wait until tomorrow.

A fond smile lifted the corners of his mouth. There was a time when his father worked every party, every event they went into, staking out potential future clients for the bank.

But why here?

Jack heard the bedroom door opening behind him. He turned, questions sprouting on his lips.

"Why all the secrecy?" The next question died before it saw the artificial light of the evening as he watched Gloria walk into the room.

She stopped dead just a few steps past the doorway, looking as surprised to see him as he was to see her.

He'd spent the better part of his allotted time at the party avoiding her. When he'd seen her coming in his direction, he'd turned away, taking a deep interest in the huge variety of hors d'oeuvres that Jose Mendoza had put out for his guests. He'd noted that she had done two U-turns on the two occasions when she'd seen him. Clearly, they were avoiding each other.

Gloria stared at him. What was Jack doing up here?

"Excuse me?" she said coldly.

"Sorry." He lifted and dropped his shoulders carelessly. "I thought you were my father."

Her eyes narrowed. That was an odd thing to say. "Why? Do I look like your father?"

Why did she have to look so damn desirable? He could feel everything inside him responding, just as it always did around her. He needed to get out.

He remained where he was. "He said he'd meet me here."

She heard the words, but they made no sense to her. "Here, in my parents' bedroom."

A humorless smile filtered over his lips for a brief second. "Yeah, does sound rather fishy, doesn't it?"

Jack started for the door, but to do that, he had to get past her. He stopped short of his goal. And her. "What are you doing here?"

"Getting a shawl for my mother."

But even as she moved toward the bureau, she realized that she'd been had. If she hadn't been so wrapped up in her own thoughts, she would have seen this coming a mile away. Especially since her mother had already done this to her once before to get her to resolve things with her sisters.

She laughed shortly and shook her head. "I smell a conspiracy." Unable to help herself, she smiled. "Your father."

Jack could get lost in that smile. "Your mother."

Could get lost in her eyes, he added.

"What the hell are they thinking?" Gloria asked, the tolerance beginning to ebb from her voice.

She jumped as the door behind her suddenly slammed shut.

The next moment her mother's voice came through the closed door. "They're thinking that maybe you should talk about the baby."

Gloria spun around, staring at the door, visualizing her mother behind it. Had Sierra talked? "You know about the baby?"

The next moment all thoughts of her mother vanished as she heard Jack demand, "What baby?"

Angry at being set up this way and cornered by her own flesh and blood, angry that this had even happened to her, Gloria turned to face him and retorted, "Your baby. Our baby." And, ultimately, her baby, she thought. Because it would be. Hers alone.

Jack's eyes shifted to her stomach. She was wearing a clingy turquoise dress that breathed with her. Her stomach was flat. "We have a baby?" he asked incredulously.

Did he think she was making this up? "In about eight months we will."

His eyes were open so wide as he stared at her, he looked like a deer caught in the headlights, she thought disdainfully.

"Why didn't you tell me?"

His voice was dangerously low. Any second, he was going to explode, she just knew it. She tried the door, but it was locked. There was no escaping this confrontation.

Damn it, Mama, why are you humiliating me like this?

"Because I just found out. And besides, it doesn't concern you."

"The hell it doesn't!"

His voice almost rattled the overhead light fixture. Taking a deep breath, Jack tried to compose himself. But there were at least a dozen emotions whirling through him, each trying to take their turn at him. And all the while, a strange sort of joy was weaving itself in and out, lighting up the darkness inside.

He looked at her stomach again. It hardly looked large enough to harbor a grape, much less the beginnings of a human being. "Are you sure?"

Because becoming defensive was a lot easier for her, she took shelter in that emotion. "What? That I'm pregnant or that it's yours?"

He saw the anger in her eyes, saw the hurt that lay beneath it. Saw echoes of himself in her defensiveness. He'd been like that, he realized. Ever since Ann had died, he'd barred every hand that reached out to him. All these years, he'd gone out of his way to keep everyone at bay.

Maybe it was time for a change.

"That you're pregnant," he answered her question tersely. "Because I know that if you are, it has to be mine."

No, she wasn't going to lower her guard, wasn't going to take solace in his words. She was going to throw them back at him. Her chin shot up as though daring him to hit her.

"And why is that?"

His eyes met hers. He wanted to hug her, to hold her in his arms and to just revel in the news she had thrown at him. A baby. They were going to have a baby. That feeling of ultimately being alone had disappeared, just like that. "Because you're not the kind of woman who fools around with a lot of guys."

The fact that he said it, that he even thought it, warmed her heart.

She struggled not to let it.

In her opinion she was way too vulnerable here and she couldn't afford to be. "And how would you know that?"

He spelled it out for her. "Logically, if you were the kind of woman who slept around, you would have been prepared. You would have offered me a condom, or been on the pill."

Jack paused, knowing if he said the next thing out loud, he would be taking a huge step. A step that, once taken, might not allow him to go back.

Making up his mind, he took it anyway. "And emotionally, I just know."

He was telling her that he felt things when it came to her. Gloria pressed her lips together, telling herself not to cry. What he said didn't change anything. In the long run, he was going to back away. Maybe offer her some financial help, but that was it. And even if he was half responsible for the condition she found herself in, she wasn't about to ask for anything. Or take anything.

"You don't have to worry," she told him quietly. "I don't expect anything."

He caught her arm before she could turn away. He didn't want to talk to her back. She needed to look him in the eye, to see that he was serious. "But I do. I expect to see my son or daughter every day."

The man was just full of surprises. "You want custody?"

"Yes." He looked at her pointedly. "Of the baby and of you."

"I'm too old for someone to have custody of me."

He looked annoyed that she was playing with semantics. "You know what I mean."

Happiness leaped inside her. He wanted her. But the next moment, logic came along to snuff out the joy. "No."

He stared at her, shaking his head slightly as if to clear his ears. "What?"

She could feel herself turning to jelly inside, not knowing how much longer she could stand firm. Gloria struggled to sound distant. "It's not a big word, Jack. I said no."

He wasn't about to let it go at that. Having made up his mind about the matter, about her, he was digging in for the duration. He had no other choice. He loved her and the baby whose existence he hadn't known about fifteen minutes ago.

"Why not?"

She fisted her hands on her hips. Was he dense? "What do you mean, why not? I'm not going to have you marry me out of pity or some misguided sense of obligation. Until you found out about the baby, you weren't even talking to me. You were going to go back to New York without so much as a goodbye. And now you want to marry me?" She was no one's charity case. "No way. Now I'm sorry if that offends your sense of pride, or honor or whatever, but—"

"Enough!" he yelled. Then, as she stared at him, stunned, he demanded, "Can you stop talking for just one damn minute?" As if to underline his request, he pointed to his watch.

He was wearing the watch she'd repaired.

Did that mean something?

God, she had to stop searching for hidden meanings in everything. If he was wearing the watch, it just meant that he liked it, not that he was wearing it because she'd fixed it for him.

"Why?" Gloria demanded hotly. "Why should I stop talking?"

"So I can tell you I love you," he shouted back at her.

She wanted to believe him. Rising up on her toes, her hands still on her hips, she jeered, "Oh, just like that."

"Yes." He was still shouting. "Just like that. From the first moment I saw you, damn it."

She felt as if she'd just taken a torpedo to her hull. His words sank in. Was he serious? One look at his face told her that he was. Her heart turned over in her chest. "You're going to need a little schooling in being romantic."

"I don't want schooling, I want you." It was time to make a clean confession. She wasn't going to believe him otherwise and he needed her to believe him. And to understand. "That's what I was afraid of."

She heard him, but she couldn't believe him. How could that possibly be true? "You were afraid of me?"

Nodding, he took her hands from her waist, one at a time, and then took her into his arms. "Afraid to admit what I was feeling. Afraid that if I did, fate would pull the rug out from under me the way it did with Ann."

And just like that, her heart went out to him. "Jack, there're no guarantees in life."

"Yes, and I'm logical enough to know that." His eyes

caressed her face as they washed over her. "I'm also human enough to be afraid of losing you."

She tilted her head, as if trying to find a way to fit the thought in. "So if you never get me, you can't lose me?"

It did sound pretty stupid when she said it out loud. "Something like that. But now there's a third person to consider." He pulled her closer, the baby a tiny seed between them. "I can't be selfish. I'm going to be a father." Feeling more love than he could ever put into words, he looked at her for a long moment. "I'd like to be a husband, as well."

She bit her lip, as afraid as he was to expose herself to more disappointment. "I don't know—"

Less than an hour ago that would have been enough to make him back away. But he was a different man now than he was half an hour ago. He dug in, then took one hell of a dive off the cliff he'd been standing on. This was for all the marbles.

"All I have to know is if you love me." He searched her face, hoping to see his answer.

She had to keep reminding herself to breathe. Air kept standing still in her lungs. "And that's all?"

"That's all." And then, because fearing that she would say no, he swung the back of his wrist against the closest bedpost. The crystal cracked. A tiny bit of glass fell on what was almost the only piece of comforter that was still exposed. "I need you to fix my watch, Gloria." And then he told her what was in his heart. "I need you to fix me."

She could feel the tears gathering inside her. Happy tears this time. "Oh, God, you make it hard to say no."

He ran his finger along her lips, already tasting them. "Then don't. Don't say no. Say yes, Gloria. Say yes. You smile when you say yes. Try it and see," he urged.

"Yes," Gloria murmured, then said it more loudly. "Yes." She laughed. "You're right." She threaded her arms around his neck, then looked over her shoulder toward the door, remembering that they hadn't been alone. Was her mother still standing out there? "Did you get all that, Mama?"

"Every word." There was pure joy in her mother's voice. "About time you were sensible."

Sense, Gloria thought as she turned back to the man who had her heart, had nothing to do with it. "Aren't you going to kiss me?" she whispered.

He secured his arms around her, pulling her closer. "For the rest of my life."

Laughter filled her. "Might make eating difficult," she teased.

"I'll find a way," he promised as he lowered his mouth to hers.

She knew that if anyone could do it, Jack could.

It was the last thought she had just before she sank into the kiss. And the four-poster. It proved to be a great deal more comfortable for lovemaking than the elevator floor had been.

Epilogue

"I don't do windows."

Christina grinned as she opened the door to her apartment wider, letting her sister in. It was the following weekend and a great deal had happened. More than some people packed into a year. In seven days, Gloria had opened her store, announced she was pregnant and then, with Jack at her side, announced she was getting married.

Which meant that she now had to pay up.

Closing the door, Christina surveyed the costume Gloria was wearing. It was the Hollywood version of what a French maid's costume should be. Christina imagined that Jack had approved of the super-high hemline.

"Nice outfit. And, yes, you will do windows." A frown appeared on Gloria's face. Christina laughed. "Don't do the crime if you can't do the time. Lucky for you I don't have a house. Now, I have a whole list of stuff for you to do." She unfurled what looked like a scroll, purely for dramatic effect.

Gloria stared at it. Every line of the two-foot roll of paper was written on. She raised her eyes to Christina's face. "You're kidding, right?"

Christina handed her the scroll. "You think this is bad, you should see Sierra's list."

Gloria looked around the modern apartment. Their tastes were similar, she thought. Clean, homey lines, not too cluttered, not too austere. "But you just moved in here, how dirty can it be?"

Christina fixed her with a look. "Correct me if I'm wrong, but aren't maids not supposed to talk back?"

"Obviously you never watched the *Brady Bunch*." She looked at the list that Christina had handed her. "This thing is incredible."

Christina shrugged nonchalantly. Half the things on there weren't going to be attended to, especially not in Gloria's condition, but she'd enjoyed coming up with the insurmountable list. "Hey, us executive types don't have time to clean."

Gloria stuffed the list into her shallow pocket. "You

know, there are cleaning services you could avail yourself of."

"I didn't say rich executive types, now did I? Besides, I'd feel too guilty paying someone to clean my place. Mama does her own work."

Gloria thought of the way her mother had plotted to get her together with Jack. If not for her, who knew how things would have wound up? "Mama is a piece of work." She smiled broadly. "The very best."

"Yeah." There was no arguing with that.

Tugging at her short skirt, Gloria braced herself. "Okay, where do you want me to start."

"With this." Christina surprised her by throwing her arms around her and hugging hard. "God, I hope you're happy, little sister."

Gloria grinned, her eyes dancing. "If I were any happier, I'd have to be two people."

"Well, you deserve it," Christina told her, feeling a little wistful because she knew she'd never be there to join Gloria in that new place she'd found. "Now, I thought you could start in here…"

Gloria groaned as she followed her sister into the kitchen.

There, next to the counter, was a bucket and every cleaning product known to man. Unopened. Christina gestured toward them, then added, "And I'd like you to whistle while you work."

Gloria gave her a look. "That wasn't part of the deal."

"Today I am the boss of you and I say it is."

With a sigh, Gloria began to whistle. Actually, she thought as she picked up a sponge and counter cleanser, she had a great deal to whistle about.

* * * * *

*Don't miss the next
The Fortunes of Texas: Reunion story,
A TYCOON IN TEXAS,
by reader favorite Crystal Green,
coming in March 2005.*

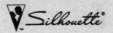

SPECIAL EDITION™

GOLD RUSH GROOMS

Lucky in love—and striking it rich—
beneath the big skies of Montana!

The excitement of Montana Mavericks: GOLD RUSH GROOMS continues

with

PRESCRIPTION: LOVE
(SE #1669)

by favorite author

Pamela Toth

City slicker Zoe Hart hated doing her residency in a
one-horse town like Thunder Canyon. But each time
she passed handsome E.R. doctor Christopher Taylor in
the halls, her heart skipped a beat. And as they began
to spend time together, the sexy physician became a
temptation Zoe wasn't sure she wanted to give up. When
faced with a tough professional choice, would Zoe opt to
go back to city life—or stay in Thunder Canyon with the
man who made her pulse race like no other?

Available at your favorite retail outlet.

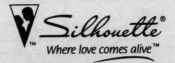

Where love comes alive™

Visit Silhouette Books at www.eHarlequin.com   SSEPL

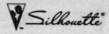

SPECIAL EDITION™

Don't miss the second installment in the
exciting new continuity, beginning in
Silhouette Special Edition.

THE
F✦RTUNES
OF TEXAS:
Reunion

A TYCOON IN TEXAS

by Crystal Green

Available March 2005

Silhouette Special Edition #1670

Christina Mendoza couldn't help being attracted
to her new boss, Derek Rockwell. But as she
knew from experience, it was best to keep things
professional. Working in close quarters only
heightened the attraction, though, and when family
started to interfere would Christina find the courage
to claim her love?

**Fortunes of Texas: Reunion—
The power of family.**

Available at your favorite retail outlet.

Where love comes alive™

Visit Silhouette Books at www.eHarlequin.com   SSEATIT

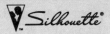

SPECIAL EDITION™

Introducing a brand-new miniseries by
Silhouette Special Edition favorite author
Marie Ferrarella

One special necklace,
three charm-filled romances!

BECAUSE A HUSBAND
IS FOREVER

by Marie Ferrarella

Available March 2005
Silhouette Special Edition #1671

Dakota Delany had always wanted a marriage like
the one her parents had, but after she found her
fiancé cheating, she gave up on love. When her
radio talk show came up with the idea of having her
spend two weeks with hunky bodyguard Ian Russell,
she protested—until she discovered she wanted Ian
to continue guarding her body forever!

Available at your favorite retail outlet.

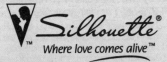

Where love comes alive™

Visit Silhouette Books at www.eHarlequin.com   SSEBAHIF

If you enjoyed what you just read,
then we've got an offer you can't resist!

Take 2 bestselling love stories FREE!

Plus get a FREE surprise gift!

Clip this page and mail it to Silhouette Reader Service™

IN U.S.A.
3010 Walden Ave.
P.O. Box 1867
Buffalo, N.Y. 14240-1867

IN CANADA
P.O. Box 609
Fort Erie, Ontario
L2A 5X3

YES! Please send me 2 free Silhouette Special Edition® novels and my free surprise gift. After receiving them, if I don't wish to receive anymore, I can return the shipping statement marked cancel. If I don't cancel, I will receive 6 brand-new novels every month, before they're available in stores! In the U.S.A., bill me at the bargain price of $4.24 plus 25¢ shipping and handling per book and applicable sales tax, if any*. In Canada, bill me at the bargain price of $4.99 plus 25¢ shipping and handling per book and applicable taxes**. That's the complete price and a savings of at least 10% off the cover prices—what a great deal! I understand that accepting the 2 free books and gift places me under no obligation ever to buy any books. I can always return a shipment and cancel at any time. Even if I never buy another book from Silhouette, the 2 free books and gift are mine to keep forever.

235 SDN DZ9D
335 SDN DZ9E

Name	(PLEASE PRINT)	
Address	Apt.#	
City	State/Prov.	Zip/Postal Code

Not valid to current Silhouette Special Edition® subscribers.

Want to try two free books from another series?
Call 1-800-873-8635 or visit www.morefreebooks.com.

* Terms and prices subject to change without notice. Sales tax applicable in N.Y.
** Canadian residents will be charged applicable provincial taxes and GST.
  All orders subject to approval. Offer limited to one per household.
  ® are registered trademarks owned and used by the trademark owner and or its licensee.

SPED04R   ©2004 Harlequin Enterprises Limited

eHARLEQUIN.com

The Ultimate Destination for Women's Fiction

Becoming an eHarlequin.com member is easy, fun and **FREE!** Join today to enjoy great benefits:

- **Super savings** on all our books, including members-only discounts and offers!

- Enjoy **exclusive online reads**—FREE!

- Info, tips and **expert advice** on writing your own romance novel.

- FREE romance **newsletters,** customized by you!

- Find out the latest on your **favorite authors.**

- Enter to win exciting **contests and promotions!**

- Chat with other members in our **community message boards!**

To become a member, visit www.eHarlequin.com today!

INTMEMB04R

Curl up and have a

Heart *to* Heart

with

Harlequin Romance®

Just like having a heart-to-heart
with your best friend, these stories
will take you from laughter to tears
and back again. So heartwarming
and emotional you'll want to
have some tissues handy!

Next month Harlequin is thrilled to bring you
Natasha Oakley's first book for Harlequin Romance:

For Our Children's Sake (#3838),
on sale March 2005

Then watch out for....

A Family For Keeps (#3843),
by Lucy Gordon, on sale May 2005

Available wherever Harlequin books are sold.

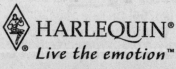

HARLEQUIN®
Live the emotion™

www.eHarlequin.com

HRHTH

SILHOUETTE Romance ®

TRADING PLACES WITH THE BOSS
by Raye Morgan
(#1759) On sale March 2005

When Sally Sinclair switched roles with her
exasperating boss, Rafe Allman, satisfaction
turned to alarm when she discovered Rafe was
not only irritating…he was also utterly irresistible!

BOARDROOM BRIDES:

**Three sassy secretaries are about
to land the deal of a lifetime!**

Be sure to check out the entire series:

THE BOSS, THE BABY AND ME
(#1751) On sale January 2005

TRADING PLACES WITH THE BOSS
(#1759) On sale March 2005

THE BOSS'S SPECIAL DELIVERY
(#1766) On sale May 2005

Only from Silhouette Books!

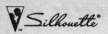

INTIMATE MOMENTS™

presents a provocative new miniseries by
award-winning author

INGRID WEAVER

PAYBACK

Three rebels were brought back from the brink and
recruited into the shadowy Payback Organization.
In return for this extraordinary second chance, they
must each repay one favor in the future. But if they
renege on their promise, everything that matters
will be ripped away…including love!

Available in March 2005:
The Angel and the Outlaw
(IM #1352)

Hayley Tavistock will do anything to avenge the
murder of her brother—including forming an
uneasy alliance with gruff ex-con Cooper Webb.
With the walls closing in around them, can love
defy the odds?

Watch for Book #2 in June 2005…
Loving the Lone Wolf
(IM #1370)

Available at your favorite retail outlet.

Visit Silhouette Books at www.eHarlequin.com   SIMTAATO